It Always Rains After a Dry Spell!

and
Other Short Tales of the
Old Southwest

Marshall Trimble

Marshall Trimble

Christmas, 1992

Published by
Treasure Chest Publications, Inc.
P.O. Box 5250
Tucson AZ 85703-0250

Design and Typesetting by
Casa Cold Type, Inc.

Cover Design by
Kathleen A. Koopman

Printed in the U.S.A.

Printing 10 9 8 7 6 5 4 3 2 1

ISBN 0-9128080-67-3

There once was a time, the old-timers tell
When for seven long years, no moisture fell.
But they didn't despair, for they knew all too well
That it always rains . . . after a dry spell!

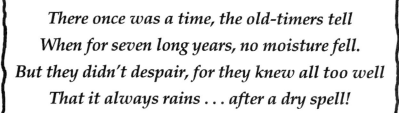

Introduction

**"If it didn't happen this way,
it could have happened this way!"**

— Mark Twain

**"If it didn't happen this way,
it should have happened this way!"**

— J. Frank Dobie

Western lore is one of America's most cherished and enduring traditions. The West attracted a legion of colorful, nonconforming men and women mavericks, most of them wandering sugarfoots. They ranged from the deserts of Arizona to the snowy ranges of Alaska. This feature alone makes them interesting and worth getting to know.

They were as big as the land itself. By the sheer power of their personalities and presence, they shaped events wherever they went, leaving behind a legacy so grand that myth and reality surrounding their lives has become hopelessly intertwined.

One of the characteristics of the newcomers to this marvelous country was the art of exaggeration. Tall tales! The West overwhelmed most and, as a result, an honest description never seemed quite enough. Legend has it the Spanish conquistadores started things off in 1540 when one gazed off into the Grand Canyon and dryly observed it'd be a "hell 'ov a place to lose a cow!"

Out West, the mountains weren't just steep, they were so steep, "a mountain goat had to shut his eyes and walk sideways!" It wasn't enough to say a man was merely bad, he was so bad that, "when he was a baby, his mama gave him some rattles to play with . . . and she left the snake attached!" A man wasn't just ugly, he was so ugly, "the flies wouldn't even light on him!" An old-timer hadn't just been around for a long time—"he was here when the Petrified Forest was just tiny seedlings!"

A place wasn't just noisy, it was "noisier 'en a jackass in a tin shed." The fella telling about a cowboy who was so drunk he couldn't hit the ground with his hat had more lollapalooza when he said the cowboy was, "so drunk he couldn't hit the ground with his hat in *five* tries!" And, how thin were Jesusita's tortillas? "They were so thin they only had *one* side!"

Tall tales are funny, wildly imaginative, interesting, and enduring. They're uniquely American and our most popular form of popular literature. And, there's some basis for truth in most tales, no matter how outrageous. The listener is led down the path of plausibility and has to figure where to get off. It's called "pulling legs attached to tenderfeet."

Webster's defines folklore as "traditional customs, beliefs, tales, or sayings preserved unreflectively among a people; hence the science which investigates the life and spirit of a people as revealed in such lore."

Folklore is deeply ingrained in all cultures. Society craves heroic figures. If it doesn't have them, it invents them.

Legends are stories that come down from the past, sometimes taken as historical though not verifiable. Some grow in the minds of people. Others are the result of events such as ghost camels in the desert and lost mines. Some have been around for so long, and are so deeply ingrained in our culture, we're no longer certain which are fact and which are fiction. Many are a combination of the two.

Writers and historians often overlook the importance of humor in a society. As a nation, humor has taken us through some mighty tough times. For that reason, Will Rogers should be considered one of the 20th century's greatest Americans. His timeless wit and wisdom is as relevant today as it was when he said it some sixty years ago.

Today, universities hold seminars on humor, trying to intellectualize and explain it rather than simply enjoying it. The same is true of many books on cowboy humor. I've tried to refrain from explaining. I just want to tell a good story and tell it as if we were sitting by a warm fireplace on a rainy winter's evening.

Tall tales and windies are like folk songs, the names and locations can be changed to fit. Ubiquitous pioneers carried these west and spread them like wild flower seeds to flourish in new surroundings. The serendipitous quest for this array of lore is something akin to searching for a needle in a haystack and finding the farmer's daughter instead!

I can't quit this introduction without mentioning some special friends. Jack Graham, commercial artist, former student, and close friend for more than twenty years, did the illustrations. He's illustrated several of my books and just keeps gettin' better and better. Thanks to Hugh Harrelson of *Arizona Highways* magazine for all his encouragement over the years.

My early mentors—Oren Arnold, Kearney Egerton, Gail Gardner, Don Schellie, Doc Sonnichsen, Roscoe Willson, and Hube Yates—are all gone now, but their rich legacy lives on in the colorful stories of Ben Avery, Joe Beeler, Bud Brown, Jim Cook, Don Dedera, Travis Edmonson, Dolan Ellis, Denny Freeman, Big Jim Griffith, Bob Hirsch, Stella Hughes, Katie Lee, Sam Lowe, Marguerite Noble, Budge Ruffner, and Maggie Wilson. Put this bunch around the fire and first liar wouldn't stand a chance. I know, I've been there with a few of 'em. They're folks I'm proud to call friends and, because of them, my life has been greatly enriched.

I can't vouch for the veracity of many of these stories. I attempted to separate the obvious tall tales into a separate section. Most of the names and places have been changed to protect the innocent . . . ahem, writer. Some are either true or have some basis for truth. Others might have been true, a few should have been true, and a couple are bald-faced lies. All are a rich part of the oral tradition in that special place we call the American Southwest. Stories about how it never rains in Arizona are slightly exaggerated, because, as any old cowboy can tell you: *It always rains after a dry spell!*

Marshall Trimble
1992

About the Author

Several years ago, Marshall Trimble was driving to a Phoenix radio station to appear on a local talk show. He had the radio in his old pickup tuned to the station and heard the host hyping his appearance by referring to him as the "Will Rogers of Arizona." Trimble was quite flattered and after the show expressed his gratitude. "Will Rogers was my idol," he drawled modestly, "but I don't deserve such a comparison."

"I know you don't," the host replied, bursting Trimble's bubble, "but if I had said 'Marshall Trimble, Arizona Historian,' most of our listeners would have switched to another station."

Marshall Trimble is a historian, many call him the dean of Arizona historians. He makes history fun. His Arizona history classes are always filled to capacity. He's taught Arizona history at Scottsdale Community College for more than twenty years. He is also director of Southwest Studies with Maricopa Community Colleges, a unique program responsible for cultural studies at ten community colleges. The award-winning author has written ten books on the state, serves on several state boards, and has seen most of the state's scenic beauty from the back of a horse.

But, there is another side to this native Arizonan, equally important. He is a popular entertainer. His homespun humor is an outgrowth of his rural roots. He claims Ashfork, the northern Arizona town he was raised in, was so small they had to "share their one horse with another community!"

His roots grow deep in the Southwest. His mother, Juanita, was born in the wooded hills of northern Arkansas and his father, Ira, was a third generation Texan from San Antonio. His great-grandfather, Sam Walker Trimble, served with a Texas cavalry unit in the Civil War and was a Texas Ranger during the Indian wars.

Trimble began his career as a folksinger in the early 1960s during the heyday of the Kingston Trio. "Our group, the Gin Mill Three, was a Kingston Trio clone from the striped short sleeve shirts, down to the pointed-toed loafers and white sox," he declares. Those years also included some time spent as a working cowboy. Both experiences developed a deep interest in the history and folklore of the Old West.

After Trimble's first book, *Arizona*, was published by Doubleday in 1977, he was in great demand as a public speaker. He drew upon his experience as an entertainer and began a new career as a storyteller and cowboy poet. Today, he is one of America's most popular speakers on Arizona and the Southwest. His many books give him credibility and his long experience as an entertainer keeps him in demand as a convention performer.

Many of Trimble's favorite stories are included in *It Always Rains After a Dry Spell.*

That talk show host's beguiling hype turned out to be prophetic. The label stuck and, today, Trimble is truly recognized as "The Will Rogers of Arizona."

Table of Contents

PART TWO: Wild & Woolly

PART THREE: As Big as All Outdoors

PART ONE

Cow Tales & Tall Tales

Down in the ghost town of Total Wreck, Arizona, lies a small cemetery. In that cemetery is a headstone that reads:

Here lies the tongue

of Prevaricator Bill.

Which always lied,

and lies here still.

CHAPTER 1

It Always Rains
After a Dry Spell!

Whenever a bunch of Arizonans gets to palaverin', tradition dictates they discuss or, more likely, cuss the cantankerous, persistent dry weather. Each prevaricator likes to claim that his or her particular area has the driest rivers, dustiest dust storms, least rainfall, or longest droughts. Get a bunch of 'em argurin' and first liar doesn't stand a chance. Some of these folks are so bad, you can't believe them even when they *say* they're lyin'. Amos Cauthen got caught tellin' the truth one time and it took him thirty minutes to lie his way out of it!"

Windjammers like to boast that their heat is a wonderful "dry heat," something that probably helps to explain why most of the rainfall is a "dry rain." I've known folks who prayed their family picnic would get rained on so the youngsters would have something to tell their grandchildren. Optimism soars and natives grab their hats or umbrellas when the weather forecaster goes out on a limb and predicts a "slight chance for brief showers." Hopeful strangers have been known to show up wearing rain slickers at *bridal* showers. Schools cancel classes on rainy days, or if classes are in session when a rain comes, teachers suspend classes so the students can go to the windows and look at the enchanting dark clouds.

For those who are reading this for college credit, the driest year in Arizona history was 1956. It rained only 0.07 inches in western Arizona. Phoenix received only 2.82 inches that year. It was so dry the bushes were following the dogs around.

Rainfall in the desert country can be awfully vagarious, too! Besides that, it can be spotty. Ezra Stump left his double-barreled shotgun outside during a storm and it rained in only one barrel.

Sometimes Mother Nature plays favorites. A few years ago, I was in my ol' pickup heading out of Zuni, New Mexico towards the Arizona border, in a driving rainstorm. I swear, the moment I hit the sign saying, "Welcome to Arizona," the pavement was dry and the sun was shining. I put the truck in reverse and backed into the rainstorm just to savor a few more rainy moments before coming home.

Now, I'm not sayin' it doesn't rain in Arizona, 'cause it always does. Back in 1905, it rained 19.73 inches in Phoenix. That year the dairy cows were giving 1% milk.

Down in Cochise County, in southeastern Arizona, lies the Sulphur Springs Valley. This arid place, where it's claimed a six-inch rain means the drops of rain were measured six inches apart, is known to locals as the "Sufferin' Springs Valley." One can go months without even seeing a cloud. Back during ol' Noah's day, when it rained forty days and nights, they only got half an inch in Sulphur Springs Valley.

Angus and Hattie Boone left their Kentucky home and set out for a new life in Gila Bend. The first thing they did was to start looking for a suitable place to live. They found an adobe house, owned by an old prospector named Milo O'Sullivan. The house looked like it would suit their needs, but before committing, Hattie looked up at the ceiling and asked, "Are you sure the roof doesn't leak?"

The old prospector got a puzzled expression on his face and then asked, "Leak *what*?"

Folks like to complain about the heat in southern Arizona, but it does get cold in some parts of the state. Temperatures dropped so low at Flagstaff last winter folks had to bring the snowmen indoors at night. You had to leave the refrigerator door open to warm up the kitchen. Mick McDuffy claimed one morning he saw a hunting dog pushing a cottontail tryin' to get him jumpstarted. And, the fur collar on Bodine Gump's winter coat grew three inches!

Up north of the San Francisco Peaks, around Cedar Mesa, there used to be a big lake—but it's not there anymore. One December day a few years ago, a flock of ducks landed on it, and moments later the temperature dropped suddenly, causin' that lake to freeze solid. Didn't hurt those ducks none. They up and took off, flappin' their wings and carried that lake right along with 'em. Far as we know, that lake's down in Mexico somewhere and now there's just another dry hole in northern Arizona.

Out near Willcox is a huge dry lake bed. Old-timers claim that at one time its sparkling blue waters matched those of Lake Tahoe. That is, until a group of German tourists held a picnic there a few years ago. They brought along several kegs of beer and a barrel full of pretzels. They sipped suds and devoured pretzels all afternoon, but when they got ready to leave, there was still half a barrel of pretzels. So they emptied the rest into the lake. Well, the fish started eating those pretzels, got so thirsty they drank up all the water. And there hasn't been enough rain since to refill it.

Speaking of fish, Arizona has a rare native species called a *"Desert Canteen"* fish. This unusual fish has a hump on its back similar to a camel, and, like the camel, uses it to store water. It has the uncanny ability to know when a water hole is drying up so it drinks its fill and then sets out across the desert in search of another water hole. They can smell water for a distance of forty miles and have been known to travel that far in search of a new home. These fish must eventually find water before their canteens run dry.

Canteen Fish shouldn't be confused with the *Desert Native Trout*, a unique species that can't swim at all and doesn't need water to survive. Avid fisherman, Bob Hirsch, a longtime friend and one who would never fib about something so serious, claims that he caught one that was so big, he took a picture and the *negative* weighed four pounds.

Desert Natives are normally found in dry riverbeds like the Agua Fria and the Hassayampa. *Desert Catfish* are also found in those dry riverbeds. Oliver Snagnasty claimed to have caught a big one one time that had fleas. It seemed reasonably intelligent, for a fish, so he took it home and trained it to catch mice.

At Verde Hot Springs, there is a place in the rocks where water comes gushing out at over a hundred degrees. Dooley Ledbetter claimed he knew the exact spot where the hot water flowed into the Verde. It was his secret fishin' hole. He said the specific gravity of the scalding water caused it to stay on top and float on a stratum three or four feet thick in that area. Dooley dropped his line down to the cold water beneath. He'd snare a trout, then lift it up slowly through the hot water cooking the fish as it passed through. He swore the fish were ready to eat by the time they were reeled in.

While on the subject of unusual desert critters, let us not forget the poor, maligned *Arizona Chip Seal.* They are the only seals that are native to the state. Chip Seals are distantly related to the larger and more familiar seals found frolicking on the California coast except they are tiny and more closely resemble grey pebbles. In fact, most people can't tell a Chip Seal from a tiny stone. They are found in abundance in dry riverbeds and are gathered in by sand and gravel companies and used for road construction. Strangely, they secrete a thick, oily substance when crushed and therein lies their value. Road construction companies murder them by the millions by dumping them on roadways then crushing them with steam rollers. The surviving Chip Seals retaliate the only way they know how—by flying up and smashing the windshields of passing cars.

Another species that has adapted well to its arid environment is the stick lizard. Its scientific name is *Crotaphytus arbo-hypothermis* or, less formally, the Arizona Limb Lizard. This durable critter carries a small stick in its mouth when scampering across the hot ground. When its little feet get too hot, the stick lizard plants the stick in the ground like a pole vaulter, then shinnies up and stays clinging to the pole until its feet cool off. Soon as those little tootsies cool down, the stick lizard climbs down the pole and goes again.

☁ ☁ ☁

Rattlesnakes are among the most feared and misunderstood of all desert critters. They play a very important part in the ecological chain by keeping the rodent population in check and are also helpful to humans. A prospector named Gassy Thompson used to tell a story of a time when a baby rattler followed him home. He did all he could to make it leave, but it wouldn't, so he turned it into a pet. He figured that a snake crawling along on the ground would have a better eye for detecting nuggets so he trained it to look for gold. The snake would signal its discovery to Gassy by rattling whenever it found a nugget. Many people doubted the story but nobody could explain why Gassy always found more gold then the other sourdoughs.

Speaking of snakes, Gassy claimed desert campers needn't worry about rattlesnakes slithering into their bedroll if they would sprinkle black pepper around the perimeter of the camp. The pepper won't keep them away but it will get them to sneezin' and they'll spit out all of their venom and their bites will be harmless.

Some of those big rattlers up around Cave Creek can pack a wallop. Ol' Gassy used to tell of a time up at Cartwright's CC outfit when a huge diamondback struck at a horse but missed and bit the wagon tongue by mistake. They had to chop off the tongue to save the wagon. The wood swelled up so big they cut it into lumber and built a three-story house. But then the swelling went down and that big house shrunk up so small they turned in into an outdoor privy.

Jug Robbins, a cowpuncher from Rye, claimed he saw a big rattler strike a cottonwood tree about ten o'clock one morning. By four o'clock that afternoon, the leaves had turned yellow and by next morning the tree had died.

During the summer of 1990, a heat wave set all kinds of records in Arizona. The climax in Phoenix came on June 26, when the mercury hit 122 degrees—that's in the shade and five feet off the ground. Temperatures went so high the weather bureau had to splice three thermometers together to get an accurate reading. A breeze came up and singed the whiskers off a prospector's face. Harvey Culpepper claims he saw a rattlesnake crawl into a brush fire just to get in the shade of the flames. Phoenicians were packin' up their suitcases and heading for Gila Bend to cool off. It got so hot the statues down at the state capitol started sweating. When a dog chased a cat, they both walked. Department stores made a quick profit selling Tammy Baker false eyelashes to women trying to screen their faces from the sun. The town of Chandler renamed its Sweet Corn Festival the Popcorn Carnival.

Folks generally tend to get irritable during a dry spell. Anyone with a dry sense of humor had best keep it to themselves. One year it was so dry over in Santa Cruz County locals threatened to string up a country singer just because he stubbornly insisted on singin' "It Ain't Gonna Rain No More" at a Saturday night dance. During a rainstorm, only one drop of rain fell and two dirt clods got into a fight over it. Wimpy Halstead claims he saw a herd of earthworms inchin' their way to a bait store so they could get a free trip to the lake.They caught a real estate salesman selling lakeshore lots on the edge of a mirage.

The Baptist preacher had to leave the country because it was no use to convert anybody. The creeks all went dry and he couldn't baptize 'em. By the time it rained enough to fill the creeks, the converts had all backslid again. It was like running down a maverick and then not having a rope to hogtie him. The churches got real civic-minded and passed a water rationing ordinance that stated henceforth, until the drought was broken, the Baptists would sprinkle, the Methodists would use a damp cloth, and the Presbyterians would issue rain checks.

Speaking of mirages, Bimbo McCready, of Salome, came up with the novel idea of brewing a fantastic light beer from a mirage. He had to quit the business after some yuppie got inebriated on the stuff and took a high dive into a dry swimming pool.

Some farmers got real resourceful during a dry spell. Down in Yuma, Jethro Sprague planted onions and potatoes between his rows of citrus. During a drought, he irrigated by scratching the onions with a pocketknife. The vapors from the onions made the eyes of the potatoes water, which, in turn, irrigated the citrus trees. The soil was so rich around Yuma that you shouldn't stand on one leg too long 'cause it would make that leg grow longer than the other and you'd end up with a limp.

Prevaricator Jones, a truthful man, who told me this story, claimed you could watch Jethro's watermelon vines crawl along the ground. Only problem was, they dragged the melons and wore them down to the size of olives. According to old-timers, Yuma was the only place in the country where you could order a martini and the bartender would ask whether you wanted it with an olive or a watermelon.

Wind is a popular topic up on the Colorado Plateau. The wind don't blow slow around Winslow or any other part of northern Arizona but it can be mighty scarce down south. My good friend, Truthful Don Dedera, tells a story of two ranchers in the Sulphur Springs Valley who got into a feud. The first cowman to settle in the valley built himself a windmill to pump water for his cattle. A few years later, another established an outfit nearby and put up a windmill. The first rancher got upset and rode over and shot down the newcomer. At his trial, the judge wondered why he resorted to such drastic measures and the cowman replied, "Well, yer honor, there just ain't enough wind in this valley for two of us!"

The case was dismissed.

Distances in the wide, open West can be deceiving. Old-timers tell of a time when an Easterner was visiting a cow ranch in southern Arizona. He kept gazing at some distant mountains and saying he'd like to hike over to them. The cowpunchers warned him those mountains were more'n fifty miles away, but he'd become accustomed to them stretching the truth. Besides, those mountains looked so close it seemed you could reach out and touch them.

Despite the punchers warning, the Easterner set out walking one morning. Later that afternoon, they got to worrying about him so they saddled up and rode out to see how he'd traveled. They found him sitting on the edge of a tiny stream, taking off his clothes. Curiously, they asked what he was doing.

"Getting ready to swim this river," he replied

"But that stream is only six inches wide," one said.

"Listen, I was already fooled *once* today by those mountains. I'm going to swim this river even if it takes all day!"

A capricious river was only a temporary setback for industrious desert-dwelling citizens. When gold was discovered in central Arizona in the 1860s, pioneer merchant Mike Goldwater moved his business to the banks of the Colorado River and helped establish the little riverport town of La Paz. One morning he awoke and found the river had changed its course, leaving the town high and dry. The unflappable merchant relocated to the banks of the Colorado again, establishing the new town of Ehrenberg.

A few years ago, the Colorado River changed its course again, this time down near Yuma. An elderly lady who had been living on the Arizona side of the river for the past fifty years looked out of her window and discovered she was now living in California. A group of media folks went out to her place to see how the old woman felt about the river relocating her to California. They were surprised to learn she was quite happy with the change.

When they asked for a statement she wiped her brow with a damp handkerchief and replied with conviction, "I don't think I could stand to spend another damn summer in Arizona anyhow."

Charlie Hunt was a skinny, old cowpuncher who ran a little greasy sack outfit south of Winslow. He was about the leanest man in those parts. Charlie was so thin he didn't even cast a shadow. One time a rattlesnake struck at him and missed *six* times.

Charlie lived alone and for years neighbors noticed that he was up at six o'clock sharp every morning. He had no radio or alarm clock. He didn't even have a rooster! Yet, ol' Charlie was always up precisely at six. When someone asked, Charlie'd just grin. Out of curiosity, a few decided to watch ol' Charlie's place one night and try to solve the mystery of this great puzzle. And sure enough they solved it. They were embarrassed by its simplicity.

Every evening at sundown, Charlie would look out towards the San Francisco Peaks and shout, "Wake up you old buzzard!" Then he'd go crawl into his bunk.

It's the gods-honest truth that Charlie's hollerin' would take hours to hit those peaks and bounce back. At six the next morning, the echo would hit Charlie's bunkhouse tellin' him to get up.

Speaking of distances and deception, mirages have fooled even the most seasoned Westerner. Heck Redondo told of a time . . . let's let him tell it:

"I was camped over in the Sulphur Springs Valley with a bunch of thirsty cows. Most of the water holes was all dried up, so I took the cattle up Dry Creek, about an hour's ride from my camp. Then I came upon this big water hole that was as fine as any you ever saw. I water'd the stock in that pond for more'n a week 'for I realized I was bein' played for a sucker. There was no water at all—it was only a meerage. But it kept the cattle from goin' thirsty!"

The original five Babbitt brothers came to Flagstaff in the 1880s and began a family dynasty. Their offspring have been multiplying in great numbers every since.

High up in the San Francisco Peaks not long ago, a citizen of Flagstaff shouted at the top of his lungs, "My name is Babbitt!"

A few minutes later, an echo retorted, "*Which* Babbitt?"

Residents down in old Cochise tell of an Eastern fellow named Smedley Bodine, who inherited a bunch of money, moved out West, and decided to try his hand at farming. He plowed some ground and planted corn one year, but it didn't rain. Same thing happened the next year and the next. But he was stubborn as an old army mule and was determined to raise a crop. So he went into Willcox and bought himself a big wagon, installed fourteen-inch sideboards on it, and loaded it full of dirt. Then he planted a crop of corn in the wagon box. Next, he hitched up a team of fast horses to the rig and hired a local cowboy named Shorty Muldoon to drive the team.

"Shorty, I've got a crop planted in that wagon," he explained, "and I want you to ride around the valley, keep your eyes peeled all the time, day and night. And when you see a cloud, drive under it fast as you can and wait. Sooner or later one of 'em's gonna let some rain fall and I want you to be there when it happens."

Sure enough, that cloud-chasing cowboy spent the entire summer driving that wagon load of dirt from one cloud to another.

This story ought to have a happy ending but it doesn't. That rich Easterner did raise a fine wagonload of corn that year, but went broke buyin' grain for the horses and axle grease to keep the wagon runnin'.

Old-timers know that sooner or later the drought will be broken. They rely on the prophetic words of an old cowman who sagely proclaimed, "It *always* rains after a dry spell!"

CHAPTER 2

If the Good Lord's Willin'

Old-timers around Prescott tell a story about a fine Christian cowman named Prosper Little, who owned a ranch in western Yavapai County. During one particularly long drought, he never lost his faith that the Lord would somehow provide. Most of his cows had already died; the rest had grazed down to bedrock and were now feeding on prickly pear cactus. His cowhands were so busy burying dead cows they hadn't had a chance to look for better grazing lands on the ranch. The outfit was faced with udder failure.

Finally, he sent one of his punchers, a fella named Slim Chance, over to look at one particular range and report on its condition. Slim rode out early, was gone all day, and got back late in the evening. Meanwhile, back at the ranch, Prosper had waited anxiously while the cowhand casually put his horse in the corral, went into the kitchen, spooned up a plate of beans, poured himself a cup of coffee, and sat down to eat.

"Well Slim," he finally inquired, "How bad is the grass up there?"

The cowboy stared at his plate and slowly replied, "I reckon it's purty bad. I ain't seen enough grass up there to build a bird's nest. The water hole's all dried up and if it don't rain real quick, I don't know what we'll do."

The Christian cowman smiled reassuringly, "I reckon the Lord will send us some rain when we need it bad enough."

The puncher took out his makin's and commenced to roll himself a quirly and said, "Well, if He don't know we need rain by now, I reckon He's a dang poor cowman."

Rufus Longacre had lived a hardscrabble life on his Powderhorn Ranch, so-called because it was as dry as the proverbial powderhorn. After some forty years of hard labor, and despite the constant state of drought, he'd built a pretty good spread.

One Sunday, Brother Riley, the Baptist preacher, came to call. Now Rufus wasn't a religious man but his wife, Bertie was. So in order to keep peace in the family, Rufus always did his best to tolerate the preacher's noon-time visits. Above all, Bertie warned him not to swear in front of Brother Riley.

After a humongous dinner of fried chicken and mashed potatoes smothered with country gravy, the preacher graciously asked Rufus to take him on a tour of the ranch. This pleased the old rancher, as he never missed a chance to show off the fruits of his years of hard toil. He showed the reverend the barn and corrals.

"My, but the Lord has certainly blessed you!" the preacher exclaimed in wonder.

Rufus frowned a little, but remembering his wife's warning, remained silent. Next, Rufus showed him the fine irrigation system on the ranch.

"Praise the Lord!" the preacher smiled, "His blessings bestowed on this place are wondrous!"

Rufus felt the hairs on the back of his red neck start to bristle as he thought of all the years of backbreakin' work he'd done by his lonesome, but held his temper.

Finally, they walked out in one of the pastures and gazed at the fine herd of cattle. Preacher Riley raised both hands toward heaven and proclaimed, "The Lord has certainly worked a miracle here."

That did it! Rufus exploded. "Well, by God," he growled, "for the last forty years or so, ol' Rufus Longacre's been pretty busy, too!"

Luther Claybaugh was a tough old codger who got kinda religious in his late years and occasionally attended church. On one of those times, the preacher was talking about love. "Is there anyone in the congregation who has not a single enemy? If there is, would you please stand up for us all to admire."

All was quiet for a few moments. Then old Luther stretched his lengthy frame and stood. Around him were quiet exclamations of admiration.

The preacher congratulated him on his Christian spirit and then asked, "How do you account for such a blessing? Tell us, what is your secret?"

Old Luther paused for a thoughtful moment then said unexpectedly, "To tell you the truth parson, I just out-lived all the SOB's."

Wiley Horner, of Punkin Center, had been an indefatigable sinner all his life. Old-timers claimed he could break all Ten Commandments in a single evening. When he'd first come to the Tonto Basin, it was no place for a Presbyterian. So, therefore, he didn't remain one. But when Wiley got old, he started getting penitent and thought it would do his soul good to be baptized. So, they took him up to the creek that ran just below the church, and there the preacher asked him to get ready to pray and to have all his sins washed away.

His wife Minnie had been pretty quiet up to this time, but she could no longer contain herself. "Holy smokes," she cried in disbelief, "you gonna try to do all that in that itty bitty ol' trickle!"

During a long drought in 1889, the Cattlemen's Association met in Phoenix and rancher Daniel Houston Ming was asked to give the opening prayer. He was, no doubt, feeling awkward at having to ask the Almighty for a favor. Dan was a salty, independent old cattleman who, normally, accepted nobody on heaven or earth as his master. But these weren't normal times. He slowly removed his hat, and gazing towards the heavens, began:

"Now Lord, I'm about to round you up for a good, plain talk. Lord, I ain't like those fellas who come bothering you every day. Why, this is the first time I ever tackled you for anything and if you will only grant this I promise I'll never bother you again. We want rain, good Lord and we want it bad, and we ask you to send us some. But if you can't or don't want to send us any, for Christ's sake, don't make it rain up around Hooker's or Leitch's ranges, but treat us all alike. Amen!"

Cotton Patch and Tuffy Rincon, a couple of retired cowmen, spent most of their time going to rodeos. The rest of the time was spent *talking* about rodeos. "Man, I sure hope they have rodeos in heaven," Cotton said one day.

"So do I," replied Tuffy.

"Let's make a deal," Cotton suggested. "Whichever one of us gets to heaven first will promise to let the other fella know if they have rodeos up there."

Sure enough, Cotton died a few weeks later. Soon after, Tuffy was sitting on the fence watching a rodeo when he thought he heard Cotton whispering in his ear. He listened very carefully and, sure enough, it was his old pal.

"I've got news for you Tuffy—some good and some bad," the heavenly voice said. "The good news is, there are rodeos in heaven."

"That's great!" Tuffy exclaimed. "I'm sure happy to know that. But what is the bad news?"

"You're ridin' ol' Midnight on Friday."

Three classic characters of the Old West—the cowboy, the gambler, and the lawyer—had crossed over the Great Divide and were met at the Pearly Gates by St. Peter himself. He looked at the cowboy first and said, "Welcome, my good man, and what can you contribute to this place?"

"Well," the cowboy drawled, "I can ride and rope. If any of your heavenly children stray from the fold, I can gather 'em up and bring 'em back."

"That's mighty fine," said St. Peter. "There's just one more question you must answer before you can enter the Kingdom of Heaven: can you spell God?"

"You bet!" said the cowboy. "Capital G-o-d!"

"That's correct," said St. Peter. "You're forgiven your many sins and can enter the Kingdom of Heaven." Next he looked at the gambler and asked, "What can you contribute?"

"I can supervise all the bingo games and make sure the House of God makes a profit."

"That's something we've needed for a long time. You, too, are forgiven your sins and can enter on the condition that you can spell 'God.' "

"That's easy!" said the gambler. "Capital G-o-d!"

Then, St. Peter looked at the lawyer and asked what he could contribute to the Kingdom of Heaven. The lawyer pondered for a moment then said, "Whenever there is a dispute, no matter how small, I can offer my services to settle it . . . ahem . . . for a small fee, of course."

"Well," St. Peter mulled that one over for a moment, then replied, "I suppose we might need someone like that."

"Does that mean I can enter the gates of Heaven?"

"There's one more thing," St. Peter said. "Spell zygapophysis!"

CHAPTER 3

Cow Camp
Cook Capers

The cow camp cook or *cocinero*, was pretty much the king of his domain. These biscuit shooters had to be resourceful enough to make a delicious cobbler out of prairie hen's eggs or take a can of pinto beans and convert it into mock pecan pie. Outfits prided themselves on the culinary skills of their cook. The first question a cowhand asked when joining a new outfit was "How's the grub?"

The Cosi, as he was called, was often the subject of jesting by the punchers, but they usually knew better than to push their luck. He always got the last laugh; like the time some of the boys from the Lazy J gave the Cosi a bath in a horse trough. He took revenge the next day by putting epsom salts in the pancake batter. Epsom salts happens to be one strong purgative and one might say the whole outfit had to take their punishment sitting down.

Some of the big outfits like the CO Bar, near Flagstaff, had a reputation for feeding good. Cowboys from other outfits used to find some excuse for stopping off around mealtime. During roundup, folks from Flagstaff used to come out to watch real cowboys work and eat some of that good CO Bar grub. It got so bad that sometimes there wasn't enough for the hands. Slick Forke was an old-time cowboy converted into a cook when his riding days were over. He was cooking for the outfit during one roundup when a group of ladies from Flagstaff showed up unexpectedly to sample his famous sourdough biscuits.

As the ladies approached the chuckwagon, Slick was busy mixing the sourdough, casually chewing on a huge wad of tobacco. His left cheek was puffed out so far it looked like he was trying to swallow a baseball. His speech thusly hindered, he could only nod a polite greeting. They pretended not to notice Slick's odious mannerism, instead they "ooooohed and aaaaahed" the distinct mouth-watering aroma of his sourdough. About that time, Slick hauled off and spit a big wad of tobacco into the mix and went on stirring as if nothing was out of the ordinary. Needless to say, the ladies found some reason to return to Flagstaff without having lunch. After that, Slick Forke didn't have so many uninvited guests showing up around mealtime looking for a free sample of his famous biscuits.

Some outfits couldn't afford to feed as well as the CO Bar. For that matter, some didn't even have a regular cook. In that case, one of the hands was designated as chief *cocinero*. These cooks weren't very creative and the food tasted like something the dog had drug in. The only way to keep the cowboys from bitching about the grub was to make the complainer change places with the cook. And since nobody wanted to cook, the punchers did their level best to tolerate the food without sayin' anything bad. Most of the time they just ate in silence, afraid that anything they said might be taken as a complaint.

Bronco La Doux told of a time he got stuck as cook after he asked whose old dirty socks the coffee had been strained through. Bronco hated cooking and did his level best to make the food taste bad enough to cause one of the waddies to complain. It was all to no avail, until one day an idea dawned on him like a thunderbolt from heaven: *Cow Pattie Pie.* Why didn't he think of it sooner? That was a surefire way to cause at least one puncher to cuss the cooking.

So, the next morning, after the punchers had gone out to the herd, Bronco headed out into the woods to find some fresh cow patties. He located several fresh mounds and gathered them up and headed back to camp. With great deliberation, he filled a large pie pan, smoothed it over, then, before placing it in the oven, covered it with a layer of white meringue.

Later that morning, Bronco removed the pie from the oven and his eyes beheld the finest looking pie he'd ever seen—dang near, but not quite, good enough to eat. If he hadn't known the contents, he'd 'ov been tempted to cut off a slice for himself. He couldn't wait to see the boys' faces that evening when they forked themselves a bite of *Cow Pattie Pie.*

That evening, the boys rode in, silently anticipating another terrible meal but determined not to complain. Bronco was so pleased with himself—he was anxious as a stud at a snortin' post—he couldn't wait for dessert. The punchers ate in their usual silence and were just about to put their plates away when Bronco sprung his surprise.

"How 'bout some dessert boys," Bronco smiled as he unveiled the meringue-covered meadow muffins.

The boys looked suspiciously at each other as Slim cut the pie in slices and dumped them on their plates. Then he stood back and waited for them to dig in, but one by one they mumbled something about not being hungry. All, that is, except for a big, hungry Swede named Ole Ander. He forked a chunk into his mouth, swished it around, then got this horrible look on his face. "Oh my gawd," he cried, his face contorted, "that's *Cow Pattie Pie!*"

He paused momentarily, looked around, then said quickly, "Ummm, and it shore is good!" And forked himself another huge bite.

CHAPTER 4

Cowboy Trials & Tribulations

"**R**iding for the brand" described a cowhand's loyalty to the outfit he rode for. But sometimes a cowboy's faith got a little overzealous. Like the time when Roscoe Farb, who ran a greasy sack outfit over on the Blue, was brought to trial in Springerville for rustling cows and selling a neighbor's prize stallion to a rancher in New Mexico. Roscoe righteously swore he was innocent of both charges and called his hired hand, Jasper Spurlock, to testify in his defense. During cross examination, the prosecuting attorney asked Jasper if his boss had told the truth.

Jasper considered the question for a moment and then replied with open honesty, "Roscoe told me he stole those cows, an' I believe him. He also told me he sold that horse over in New Mexico. I believe that, too! Roscoe always tells the truth and if he said he didn't do it, by God, I believe he's tellin' the truth!"

Cowboys could be kind-hearted to a fault. Bat Guano was as bad a desperado as ever rode the owl hoot trail, mean enough to eat off the same plate with a rattlesnake. He swore he'd planted so many men in the ground that he'd quit counting.

One night in Tombstone, Bat killed a man in a barroom fight and was brought to trial. Bat claimed self-defense even though the victim was unarmed. He was nervous as a tomcat in a room full of rockin' chairs, figuring they'd hang him anyway because of his past transgressions. But, his hopes brightened considerably when he learned one of the members of the jury was a cowboy.

"Hold out for manslaughter," Bat pleaded. "If you'll do me this one favor, I promise I'll never get in trouble again."

The cowboy felt sorry for old Bat Guano and promised he'd do what he could. Sure enough, the verdict came in and it was manslaughter.

Bat jumped out of his chair, ran over to the cowboy and threw his arms around him. "You did it!" he cried enthusiastically. "How can I ever thank you enough. You must have had a hell of a time convincing 'em."

"I shore did!" the cowboy exclaimed. "They all wanted to acquit ya!"

Bobby Jack Farley was up before the judge in Dudleyville on a non-support charge for his wife and eleven children. After the judge listened to the evidence, he looked at the defendant and said, "Bobby Jack, you haven't done right by your wife and kids. I'll tell you what I'm going to do. I'm going to give them 400 dollars a month."

"Why, thank ya judge!" Bobby Jack replied gratefully. "That's mighty kind. And I'll tell you what. I'll chip in a few dollars now and then, too!"

A few years ago the northern part of Yuma County split off and formed a new county, called La Paz. Hackamore Hanarahan, an old cowman in the northern part of the new county, came into town with a handful of legal problems. He was in a big hurry so he asked the first person he met, Jasper Coogan, "Do you have any criminal lawyers in La Paz?"

"We shore do," Jasper replied unhesitatingly, "but we've never been able to convict any of 'em yet!"

Cowboy Billy Lucky took his lawyer Dewey Cheetum, senior partner with the law firm, Dewey Cheetum and Howe, out camping. They were all loaded down with backpacks, climbing up a narrow trail when they came face to face with a huge grizzly bear.

The lawyer peeled off his backpack, reached inside and pulled out a pair of expensive running shoes and started putting them on.

"What're yuh doin'?" Billy wanted to know.

"I'm going to make a run for it," the lawyer replied.

"But yuh can't outrun a grizzly bear."

"I don't have to outrun the bear," the lawyer said with a sinister grin, "I just have to outrun you!"

Cowboys were also known for their open honesty. Back during his younger days, Slim Chance was brought before a crusty old Arizona judge on a charge of horse stealing. His Honor was a real stickler for proper court-room procedure and these uncurried cowhands made him frustrated as a woodpecker in the Petrified Forest. As the proceedings were about to formally begin, he looked down at Slim and asked inquiringly, "Are you the plaintiff or the defendant?"

Slim looked up at the bench with a puzzled expression and replied matter-of-factly, "Judge, I'm the one that stole the horse."

A lawyer in town who had just arrived from Philadelphia took it upon himself to defend the young cowpoke. As things stood, Slim had no more chance than a one-legged man in a kickin' contest. He knew he'd have to go around the facts of the case, (Slim was riding the plaintiff's horse when apprehended.) So the lawyer paraded the lad's poor old widowed mother in front of the jury. Then he introduced Slim's wife and kids. Finally, he put his arm around Slim's bony shoulders and asked pleadingly, "Does this look like the kind of man who'd steal a horse?"

Apparently the jury thought not for they returned a verdict of innocent.

Before dismissing the charges, the judge brought Slim up once again and asked if he had anything he'd like to say to the court. Unabashed, the young man grinned and asked, "Judge, do I get to keep that horse?"

A few minutes later, as he was leaving the courthouse, a friend walked up and with a puzzled look asked, "Slim, I watched that whole trial and I'm kinda confused. Did you, or did you not, really steal that horse?"

"Well, I sure thought I did," he speculated, "but after listening to that there lawyer, now I ain't so sure!"

Speaking of Slim Chance, he claimed he was a bronc rider who'd never been thrown, lookin' for a bronc that'd never been rode. Old-timers swore Slim could ride anything that wore hair. One time, at the Williams rodeo, he drew Chingadero, a big black horse that had never been rode. Slim bet all his money on himself and was determined to ride that critter for eight seconds. When Slim climbed into the saddle and they opened up the chute, ol' Chingadero just plumb quit the earth. He tore off into the sky for all he was worth. He was twistin' and turnin', havin' wall-eyed fits, his hind feet was perpendicular and his front ones was in the bits. You could see the tops of mountains under that Chingadero horse every jump. That buckin' bronc sunfished all over the arena with Slim spurrin' him all the way.

Then Slim astonished the crowd by takin' his free hand and rollin' himself a smoke. Finally, ol' Chingadero hit on all fours, went up on high, came down on his hind legs, then did a backflip, landing atop Slim and burying him in a cloud of dust. This all happened in less than four seconds!

Several cowboys jumped off the fence rail and rushed to his aid. "Take it easy, Slim," one yelled reassuringly, "we'll help ya up!"

"Like hell ya will," Slim snorted indignantly, spitting out a mouthful of dirt, "help ol' Chingadero up. I'm still in the saddle!"

Slim wasn't a bit short on confidence either. One time when jobs were scarce in Yavapai County, he headed for the tall timbers south of Flagstaff looking for a job. He stopped at a lumber camp near Happy Jack and asked the foreman if he was hiring. The foreman, a big strapping man, looked down at Slim and asked if he'd had any experience cutting down tall trees.

"Shore have!" Slim declared. "Where?" the foreman inquired.

"Well," Slim drawled, "have you ever heard of the Sonoran Forest?"

"Now hold on a minute," the foreman corrected, "don't you mean the Sonoran Desert?"

"It is now!" Slim grinned enthusiastically.

A Tonto Basin cowpuncher named Rocky Coffee, was out of a job and someone in Payson told him the old bear hunter, Caleb Johnson, was looking for a partner. So, he headed out to Caleb's cabin and sure enough, found himself a job.

"You ever hunted bear before?" Caleb asked.

"No," Rocky replied, "but I ain't afraid of anything that wears hair!"

So Caleb went for the gear and returned later with a shotgun, an old hound named Cooter, and a pair of handcuffs. "Well, let's go!" he said.

"Just a minute," Rocky said with a puzzled expression. "I savvy the dog and shotgun, but what're the handcuffs for?"

"I forgot to tell you," Caleb replied, "dead bears ain't worth any money. I ketch 'em alive and sell 'em to zoos. Now this is how we do it. Cooter finds a bear and trees it. I climb up and shake it loose. When that bear falls to the ground, ol' Cooter runs up and bites it on the private parts. That dog is a bitin' fool. Once he grabs on, ain't hardly no way he'll turn loose. That ol' bear will rear up on its hind legs and go 'oooooow' and reach down to protect itself with both its front paws. That's when you run up and slip the handcuffs on it. You got it?"

"Just one more thing," asked Rocky, "what's the shotgun for?"

"That's just in case the bear shakes *me* out of the tree. You shoot ol' Cooter!"

33

Speaking of Caleb and bears, he used to tell a story of a time when he ran across a big bear up on the Mogollon Rim, near Pinedale. But, let's let Caleb tell it in his own words:

"I was up there gatherin' wild strawberries one June when this ol' mama bear come roaring out of the brush. I didn't have my gun, so I took out running for dear life. I ran up and down that Mogollon Rim several times but that bear just kept comin'. Finally, we got to the White River and I crossed over on the ice. That bear got to slippin' on the ice and I got away."

At this point, a listener would invariably ask, "But, Caleb, how could you have crossed the ice in June?"

"Well, it was like this," he would reply, "we done a whole heap of runnin' and by this time it was the middle of December."

Caleb told another story of a bear chase, this one over near Springerville. Again, let's let him tell it:

"This ol' sow bear caught me unarmed in a big open meadow. She was a fierce one and was about to get my hide. I was runnin' for all I was worth and plenty skeered. I run about ten miles before I come to a single tree, and it had only one branch—and that was thirty feet off the ground. Well, I got to that tree and made a desperate jump for that branch."

Caleb would always pause and wait for some greenhorn to ask, "Did you catch that limb?"

"No!" he drawled, "but I caught it on the way down!"

Caleb had lots of bear stories. He told of another time when he got treed by a whole pack of grizzlies. He sat up in that tree for several days hoping they'd get bored and leave. During that time, Caleb had nothing to eat except a bar of soap he was carrying. He claimed after that experience, he never did care for the taste of soap.

After ten days, all the bears had left except for two stubborn old sows. A couple of days later, they shuffled off down towards the creek. Caleb waited a suitable time before coming down and just as he was making his descent, the two sows reappeared. Caleb noticed, to his horror, they had a large beaver in tow, with the clear intent of making that critter chew down Caleb's tree.

"What happened next?" the anxious listener asked.

"Well, son," Caleb replied, "they kilt and et me!"

Back during the days of prohibition, Paddy O'Brian, a Cochise County cowboy, was stopped at the customs station at Naco, Arizona, after a brief visit to Naco, Sonora. The customs officer looked into his saddlebags and pulled out a large jug. "And what might you have in the jug, Paddy?" he asked.

"That, my friend, is a bottle of holy water that I am bringing back to me loved ones."

The customs officer pulled out the cork and sniffed the contents, then hefted the jug and took a snort. "Water, did you say?" he sputtered. "Why, that's whiskey, and mighty strong whiskey at that."

"Well glory be!" cried Paddy. "Another miracle!"

A few days later Jake and Roney were discussing Paddy's dilemma:

"I heard the judge gave Paddy thirty days in the hoosegow," said Jake.

"What's the charge?" asked Roney.

"No charge!" says Jake. "Everything's free!"

The president and board of directors of the cattlemen's bank in Springerville were named as pallbearers in the will of old Henry Hanratty when he finally cashed in his chips. Henry died broke, owing the bank a considerable amount of money. "They have been wonderful creditors," the will said, "and I would like to have them carry me to the end."

CHAPTER 5

Cowboys in Town

Back in the early days, when cowboys came to town, one of the first things they did was to purchase some new duds at the general store. It's no different today. Bimbo McCready came into Flagstaff a while back and the first thing he noticed was some tourist wearing a pair of those exotic alligator boots. Bimbo decided he had to have a pair, so he hightailed it over to Babbitt's. When the clerk said they would cost $650, Bimbo decided it'd be cheaper to take a train to Florida and get a pair on his own. So, he bought a ticket on the Santa Fe and headed east.

Upon arriving, he headed out to the Everglades where he came upon a big old alligator sunning himself. When that Alligator saw that cowboy coming towards him, he headed for the deepest part of the swamp. Bimbo tore out after him with a determined look. He jumped into that swamp and climbed on that gator's back. That gator took Bimbo down to the deepest part of that swamp and tired to drown him. They rolled over and over till finally Bimbo jerked out his piggin' string and hogtied that gator's jaw, clamping it shut. Then he dragged it to shore. He flipped that ol' gator onto its back, examined it and muttered disappointedly, "Wouldn't yuh know it! I picked a barefooted one!"

☁ ☁ ☁

Waddie Culpepper came into Holbrook for a spree after three months keeping company with cows. As he was walking down Center Street towards the Bucket of Blood Saloon, a couple of tough-looking thugs jumped him. Waddie fought like a wildcat, kicking, biting, and gouging his opponents for all he was worth. Finally, they pinned him to the ground and turned his pockets inside out—and found only three wrinkled dollar bills.

The two thugs stared at each other in amazement, then one turned to Waddie and said, "You must be crazy. You put up a fight like that for *three* bucks?"

"Hell no!" Waddie declared. "I thought you was after the 200 that was in my socks!"

☁ ☁ ☁

Hortense Greever was the local spinster and town busybody in Springerville. She was well known for her high-toned ways. One day she loudly accused Stumpy Chapman of spending too much time in the local saloons. "I observed his horse outside the Silver Spur," she righteously declared, "at eleven o'clock last night!"

Late the next night, Stumpy tied his horse to Hortense's front gate. It was still there the next morning . . .

Lutie Spurlock cowboyed around northern Arizona for a few years before deciding to take a job in town selling furniture. He was real proud of his new job as a furniture salesman and he was pretty good at it. Lutie also wanted to mix in the social circles in town but wasn't having much luck with the ladies. He hadn't spent much time around women and was pretty shy in their presence. In fact, he'd much rather chase a wild cow through low-limbed brush than try to make social conversation with a woman.

Then one day he got up the courage to ask Bobbie Sue Grimsby, a new girl in town, for a date. Since she was new, and didn't know anybody, she readily accepted. Lutie couldn't believe his good fortune. The only problem is, he goes over to pick her up and finds she has a bad case of laryngitis. She can't say a word, not even a whisper. But, Lutie is resourceful. He gets her a pencil and piece of paper. "So, what would you like to do?" he asked.

She draws him a picture of a beefsteak. Lutie gets the idea real fast and he takes her out for steak and beans. Then Lutie says again, "So, what would you like to do now?"

She draws a picture of an ice cream cone. So, he takes her to the local ice cream parlor and buys her an ice cream cone. Nothin' difficult about this he figures.

As Lutie is walking Bobbie Sue home, she takes his hand and squeezes it real tight. He's starting to get nervous, wondering what to say next. When they get to her front porch he once again asks, "What would you like to do now?"

She draws a picture of a bed. Lutie looks at her in amazement, saying, "How did you know I was in the furniture business?"

Some of the old hands had trouble adjusting to modern technology. Cliff Hanger, a cowman over in Nutrioso, told of a time while driving his pickup over to Springerville to get some mechanical work done he saw an old cowpuncher standing beside the road waiting for a ride.

"Goin' to Springerville, mister?" the old man asked hopefully. "Sure am," Cliff replied, "but before you get in would you stand out in front of the pickup and tell me if these signal lights are working?"

The puncher obligingly did as he was asked and, when Cliff pulled the lever, he announced, "They're working." Then, with a puzzled expression, "No they ain't working . . . wait, they're working . . . now they ain't."

Those old-time cowboys were mostly out of place in the world of life's amenities. Mention Jacuzzi to one of 'em and he thought you were talking about a Senator from New Jersey. One time a Tonto Basin cowboy named Rowdy Cline checked into a brand new hotel in Phoenix and was thunderstruck when they charged him $2.50 for a room. Grudgingly, he paid, but when the bellhop led him to the elevator and opened the door, the cowboy drew the line. "Hold it right there," he snorted with conviction. "There ain't enough room in there to cuss out a cat without gettin' hair in yer mouth! I ain't gonna pay $2.50 for no dinky room like that."

Lee Roy Raley, who ranched up on the Blue, gathered up his family and brought them into Phoenix for their first stay in a big city hotel. Lee Roy's wife Melba had gone into the gift shop, leaving him to watch the kids. They'd never seen an elevator before so they watched with great interest as an elderly, rather heavyset woman got in and the door closed. They watched as the numbers above the door went 2-3-4-5 then stopped. Then, they went 4-3-2-1 and the door opened. This time a lovely, young lady stepped out.

"Hey Pa!" Elmo, the oldest cried, "did you see that?" "I shore did!" Lee Roy replied enthusiastically. "Let's go get yer ma and put her in there."

Willard Hoskins, a grizzled old cowman, from up on the Blue River was elected as representative to the Arizona legislature from Greenlee County. He'd spent all his life out in the rough country and had seldom been to town. He checked into the old Adams Hotel in Phoenix and, on his first night in town, a banquet in his honor was thrown by a group of lobbyists. Willard was a giant of a man with a strong, robust personality, but was generally slow to anger.

The first course was consommé. Willard looked puzzled, but consumed it. Then, someone passed him a bunch of celery. That, too, he ate. Then a waiter put a broiled lobster in front of him. Willard turned red, then rose and said, "Gentlemen, I drunk the dishwater, and I ate the bouquet, but I'll be damned if I'll eat this here bug!"

A rugged old cowman named Murphy Blanford walked into the Adams Hotel in Phoenix at the height of the season and was told no rooms were available.

"There's got to be a room," Murphy roared, "there always is."

"Sorry sir," the clerk insisted, "but we have no rooms available."

"Look," said Murphy, "if you heard President Roosevelt was coming, you'd find a room. Right?"

"Well, I guess if the president was coming," the clerk said with conviction, "we'd have to find a room."

"Well, Mr. Roosevelt can't come," Murphy declared, "so let me have his room."

☁ ☁ ☁

Arlie Cogburn cowboyed around northern Arizona most of his life, but the brutal cold winters finally got to him. It happened one cold winter day north of Flagstaff when he looked at his pocket watch and the two hands were rubbing together to keep warm. So, he quit cowboying and asked for a job as desk clerk at the Arizona Hotel in Ashfork. He admitted he'd never worked a town job before but the owner, Hadley Hicks, decided to give him a chance. "How much does it pay?" Arlie asked.

"I'll pay you what you're worth," Hadley replied.

"I won't work that cheap!" Arlie protested.

Well, they finally worked out a deal and, about an hour after Arlie started work, the phone rang. He picked up the receiver, said, "Arizona Hotel," listened for a moment, then said, "yup, you can say that again!" and hung up.

A few minutes later, the phone rang again. Arlie once more lifted the receiver. "Arizona Hotel . . . yup, it shore is!" and hung up again.

The third time the phone rang, Arlie was starting to get impatient. "Arizona Hotel . . . gol dang it, I know it is. You don't have to keep tellin' me!"

By this time, the owner's curiosity was aroused. "Arlie," he declared, "you aren't supposed to be using the telephone for personal use." "I ain't!" Arlie replied. "Then who are you talking to?"

"Sure beats me, boss. I pick up the phone. Someone says 'It's long distance from Austin, Texas,' and I keep tellin' 'em, 'It shore is!' "

New technology might have dumbfounded them, but they did have a lot of savvy on practical matters. Such was the case back around the turn of the century when a CO Bar cowboy named Charlie Spurlock came into Flagstaff and decided to go see one of those newfangled motion pictures at the Babbitt's Opera Hall.

On this particular evening, a feature was playing which showed a group of shapely young ladies out in the countryside preparing to disrobe and jump into a swimming hole. Just about the time they got down to the bare essentials, a freight train came roaring by and obscured the view. By the time the train passed and the camera focused on the ladies once again, they were submerged up to their pretty necks.

Charlie quickly sized up the situation and headed for the ticket office where he asked to purchase tickets for the next six performances.

"What on earth do you want with six more tickets?" the cashier asked. "They will all be for the same movie."

"Now ma'am," he replied matter-of-factly. "I don't know anything about these new motion pictures. But I do know something about freight trains. Sooner or later one of 'em's gonna be late and I aim to be there when it happens."

Shorty Riggins had been branding and doctoring cattle in the Tonto Basin all week so he decided to ride into Punkin Center one Saturday night and attend the weekly dance at the school house. He walked bodaciously up to the new schoolmarm, Prunella Buttrum, a proper Eastern lady who'd just moved into the area, and asked her to dance. Prunella was so straight she wouldn't even allow her students to do improper fractions in class. She considered cowboys, in general, to be a rather sorry lot of unchurched and unwashed reprobates. During the dance, Prunella wasn't very talkative so Shorty decided to loosen her up with some polite conversation. "I'm not a real good dancer," Shorty said conversationally, "I'm a little stiff from branding."

Prunella gave him a look that could turn sweet milk to clabber and replied coldly, "Quite frankly, it really doesn't matter to me where you come from!"

Pete Glover had just lost his wife of thirty years, when a sweet-smelling note arrived from his neighbor, Biddy Snodgrass. Biddy's husband had run off years ago and since then she'd been aggressively trying to snare another mate. She wasn't much to look at, the only man who considered her a ten was a shoe salesman. Biddy was also starting to get a little long in the tooth. Nowadays, the only man chasing her was father time.

"I would like to take the place of your deceased wife!" the note said. Pete wrote back: "It's fine with me, if you can arrange things with the undertaker!"

At the National Cattle Growers convention a few years back, a group of cattlemen went out to a fancy steakhouse in Phoenix for dinner. When the waitress came around, each cowman ordered his favorite cut of beef. That is, until the last one, Billy Bob Neely, spoke up. He ordered lamb chops.

The rest of the bunch was startled by this heresy from such a venerable cowman and one asked how come.

"Eat the durn things up and get rid of 'em," Billy Bob explained straight-faced. "That's my theory!"

A Texas cowpuncher named Bobby Joe Buckstitch considered himself the best pistol shot in the whole Southwest. Naturally, he was taken back a bit when he was told there was a fella over in Willcox, Arizona named Jubal O'Reilly, who also claimed the title. So, he rode the train to Willcox looking for this O'Reilly fella. Bobby Joe found Jubal sitting lazily outside the Railroad Saloon. His hat was pulled down over his eyes. Bobby Joe took a seat next to him saying, "I hear tell you're claimin' to be the best shot in the Southwest. But you cain't be 'cause I am and I'm aimin' to prove it right now!"

"How you aimin' to do that?" Jubal grunted.

Bobby Joe drew his six-shooter. "See that horsefly over there. I'm gonna blow him right out of mid air!" The pistol roared and sure enough, the horsefly disintegrated into a million pieces.

Jubal watched with mild interest then drew his revolver. "See that other horsefly?" His six-gun roared, but when the smoke cleared, the horsefly was still flitting about.

"You missed!" Bobby Joe sneered, "I guess that makes me the best pistol shot in the Southwest!"

"Guess again!" Jubal said as he pulled his hat down and resumed his slumber.

"I reckon I am," Bobby Joe opined, "my horsefly is dead and yours is still flyin'."

"He may be still flyin'," Jubal answered mildly, "but he ain't ever gonna reproduce agin!"

Charlie Dunlap was probably the most diplomatic man to ever run a cow business in Arizona. Eastern born and bred, he was a graduate student at Yale when he inherited a cow ranch in Skull Valley. He hadn't been there long when he discovered a neighbor, Ornery Hertz, was rustling his cattle and stamping his own brand on their hides.

Charlie was about to turn matters over to the law, but his other neighbors warned him that Ornery was so bad that when he was a baby his mother gave him some rattles to play with—ahem—and she left the snake attached. "In other words," they said, "he's liable to give you lead poisoning if you call in the law."

Charlie figured gentle diplomacy was the best way to handle Ornery. He typed his warning letter thusly: "Dear Ornery, I'd appreciate it if you would stop leaving your hot branding irons out where my stupid cows can sit down on them!"

Shorty and Slim were up to their usual game of "first liar hasn't got a chance." Shorty started it by claiming that one time he was sitting in camp by his lonesome having a coffee when a huge silvertip grizzly approached him menacingly. "I just waited till he got real close then I tossed that cup of coffee in his face. He lit out like a skeered rabbit."

Slim pondered that story for a moment, then drawled, "Well Shorty, I reckon that story has to be true, 'cause a few minutes after that happened I was ridin' round the side of a hill and I came upon this grizzly. And, as is my habit, I stopped to stroke his muzzle. It was still wet and smelled of coffee!"

One Valentine's Day, Dudley Van Dorn, of Clay Springs, bought his wife, Imogene, a dyed skunk coat. She held up the coat and asked, "How can such a pretty coat come from such a foul-smelling critter?"

"Imogene," Dudley cried indignantly, "you never was much for gratitude, but I do deserve a little more respect!"

Cloyd Pringle was braggin' to Buck Tyree one day. "I'm proud of my daughters," he said, "they're kinda common-looking but I want to see them comfortably married. I've saved a few dollars so they'll have some money to take into the marriage, sorta sweeten up the pot, I reckon.

Little Maude is twenty-five years. I'll give her $1,000 when she marries. Daisy Mae won't see thirty-five again. I'll give her $3,000. And the man who'll have Lizzie, who is well over forty, will get $5,000 with her."

Buck reflected for a moment and asked pleasantly, "Cloyd, you don't happen to have one about fifty, have you?"

Back in the early days, the old Butterfield Overland stageline used to run from Tucson to Lordsburg, New Mexico. One day, a cowboy approached the stage driver and said he was broke but wondered if he could work for his passage to Lordsburg. The driver looked him over and said, "Sure, you can ride shotgun!"

"What's that?" the cowboy asked.

"You sit up here on top of the stagecoach with me and watch out for bad guys."

"I think I can handle that," the cowboy replied and climbed aboard.

A few hours out of Tucson, the driver said, "Crawl up on the back of the stage and see if anybody's following us."

The cowboy did as he was told and far off in the distance he saw a tiny figure on horseback. He went back to the driver, and spreading his thumb and forefinger about an inch apart, said, "There's someone followin' us and he's only about this high."

"No problem!" the driver replied, unconcerned. "We'll check on him agin in the morning."

The next day the cowboy crawled across the back of the stage again and stared off into the distance. The figure was still following and looked much larger. Crawling back, the cowboy spread both hands two feet apart and said, "He's about this big now."

"No problem!" said the driver, still unconcerned. "We'll check him tomorrow."

The next morning the cowboy started to crawl back again and was startled to see the desperado climbing up the back of the stage.

"Where is he now?" the driver asked. "He's on top of the stage!" the cowboy shouted excitedly.

"Well, shoot him!" the driver roared.

"I can't!" the cowboy objected.

"Why?" the driver demanded.

"'Cause," the cowboy replied, holding up his thumb and forefinger about and inch apart, "I've known 'em since he was only about this high!"

49

CHAPTER 6

The Amazing Case of the Corpus Delicti Cyanide Mill

If you stood outside the entrance of your nearest shopping mall with a clipboard in your hand and asked people who invented the cyanide method of extracting gold from rock, most would quickly point out that it was first done by two Scottish chemists back in the late 1890s. Right? Wrong!

According to "Non-Assessable" Smith, a well-known literary prodigy in the art of prevarication around the turn of the century, it was his old partner Bill Bolger who invented the cyanide process one hot summer day down in Cochise County. It all happened quite by accident, but then don't most great discoveries?

One hot summer day back in the 1880s, Smith left his partner in camp sleeping off a hangover and went out prospecting in the Dragoon Mountains. A peddler wandered into camp, woke Bill up, and sold him a hatful of fresh "hen's" eggs. Now fresh eggs were scarce as horseflies in December and Bill didn't even wait to start a cookfire. He cracked a few on a flat slab of granite and fried them over-easy. Being a good partner, he generously saved some for his partner.

By the time "Non-Assessable" Smith returned to camp, Bill was suffering from a severe stomachache. Smith jumped on his mule and rode over to Benson to fetch a doctor, but by the time they got back, poor Bill was dead and getting stiffer by the minute. The doctor made a quick examination and said Bill was "ossified." Smith agreed, saying his partner was powerfully addicted to ardent spirits and was ossified most of the time.

"No, I don't mean stoned," Doc replied, "he's turning to stone. You say he had a bellyache? What's he been eating?"

Smith pointed out the fresh eggs, which Doc quickly examined and declared, "These are not hen's eggs, they're Gila monster eggs and they're full of cyanide."

It seems that the granite rock Bill used as a solar-frying cookstove was full of gold. The gold was absorbed by the cyanide which he'd eaten. By the time they got ready to load Bill in a pine box, he weighed over 1,600 pounds, and it took twelve men to lift him. Smith decided to delay the funeral and take Bill over to Tombstone and have him assayed. The tests showed he was 95% pure gold.

Needless to say, Smith canceled the funeral, took Bill back to camp and stored him in a mine shaft. For quite some time afterward, anytime Smith needed money, he'd slice a piece off his old partner's carcass and cash it in at the trading post in Dragoon.

CHAPTER 7

A Baseball Windy

Junior Salazar is a name few Arizonans will quickly recall, but back in the 1950s, he was one of northern Arizona's finest baseball players. In those days, every community along Route 66 had a baseball team known affectionately as the "town team." Games were played on dusty, rocky fields, usually in horrendous windstorms. Small children were tethered to stakes with rope lest they blow away. Sometimes the games were delayed temporarily by a wild, blowing stampede of tumbleweeds. Spectators watched the game from the comfort of their cars, parked on the outskirts of the playing field.

Most of the players were high school "has beens" or frustrated "wannabes" who'd never lost their love for the game and were trying to squeeze one more year from an arthritic arm or play on legs that had lost most of their spring. Many spent the hours before the game loading up on whatever alcoholic beverage suited them and were quite mellow by the time the umpire called "play ball."

Junior Salazar was the exception to all this. Unlike the others on his team, the Winslow Roadkills, he neither drank nor smoked during the game. He actually practiced during the week and warmed up before games, something quite rare among that breed of ballplayers. Junior's destiny was determined when, as a toddler, his daddy gave him a bat and ball and declared he'd one day be a major leaguer.

Granted, some of the tales that are still being told by old-timers in the towns along Route 66 tend to be exaggerated, but it is a matter of fact that Junior was possessed with a blazing fastball. The term "throwing aspirin tablets" is believed to have been first used in describing Junior's hurling. Old-timers claim that one stormy afternoon in a game against the Holbrook Hashknives, he pitched seven innings in a driving rainstorm and never got the ball wet.

Although Junior was a great pitcher at that level, he wasn't eccentric enough to be a hurler in the major leagues; besides, he nearly ruined his arm throwing curve balls against the wind. So, Junior took up catching. And his real chance to make a big show was at that position.

Not only was Junior a great athlete, he was an unabashed student of the game. Long before television color men were providing detailed analysis for the novice at home, he was always figuring out ways to get an edge on his opponents. One day he discovered a way to use the elements in northern Arizona to his advantage.

Junior's hometown, Winslow, was dreadfully misnamed. The wind never blew slow in Winslow. The windy season began around the first day of January and quit around the last of December. A stranger rode into town one day and asked a resident, "Does the wind blow this way all the time?" "No, sometimes it blows from the other way!" was the straight-faced answer.

Old-timers like to recall the day it stopped blowing for a moment and all the cows fell down. Locals claim the fella who designed the Leaning Tower of Pizza got his basic training at Winslow. Dentists couldn't make a living in Winslow because when folks wanted their teeth cleaned, they just grinned into the prevailing wind and sandblasted the tartar off. At Winslow's ballpark, they didn't use a flag to gauge the wind out in center field, they used a logging chain. When the town was established in the 1880s, it was only about ten miles east of Flagstaff, but the winds keep pushing it eastward. Scientists claim that sometime in the next century, Winslow will be located in New Mexico.

As Junior studied the elements, he noticed that the wind almost always blew from left field across to center. Catchers trying to throw out base runners had little success because the ball was always blown into right field. It wasn't at all uncommon for Navajo horsemen clear up in the Painted Desert to find baseballs lying half-buried in the sand.

Junior revolutionized baseball on the Colorado Plateau one windy day by throwing the ball to *third* when a runner was trying to steal second. The wind picked up the ball and carried it into second base, actually increasing its velocity along the way. During that amazing 1953 season, Junior Salazar threw out every runner who challenged his unerring throws.

Major league scouts from all over the country were excited about this baseball phenomenon from northern Arizona who never allowed a runner to steal and, although they'd never seen him play, sought to sign him.

But it was the Cubs and White Sox, both from—you guessed it—the Windy City, who were his most ardent admirers. "Junior Salazar," they proclaimed enthusiastically, "was a natural for Chicago." The bidding war between the Cubs and White Sox was highly competitive, but the Cubs eventually won. The kicker was when they threw in a brand new '53 Nash convertible as an added perk. The only other person in Winslow who owned such a flamboyant auto was Geathur Burrage, owner of the Texaco gas station and president of the local sports car club. It looked for a time like Junior Salazar was destined for a life of fame and fortune.

And speaking of fortune, it was at this time that *Ol' Dame Fortune* started dealing from the bottom of the deck. You see, Junior was accustomed to throwing baseballs up on the Colorado Plateau and there's no other place on earth where the wind blows that hard. He'd learned to use the windage so well in these extreme conditions that he couldn't adjust his throwing to normal weather—the kind that is found in most major league cities.

His worst moment came in that first game when the Cubs were playing the Giants in the old Polo Grounds. The first time a base runner tried to steal second, Junior automatically threw his 98 mph fastball to third. The ball sailed past the surprised third baseman and bounced off the left field wall, allowing the runner to score easily. The same thing happened the next time a runner tried to steal. To those spectators, it seemed that Junior was throwing to the *wrong* base. The New York fans hooted and howled with delight at poor Junior's misfortune until he finally lost all his confidence.

The Cubs tried using Junior for home games only, but the wind in Chicago was meek when compared to the Colorado Plateau. In the end, they had no choice but to buy him a one-way railroad ticket back to Winslow.

After that unfortunate experience, Junior sorta gave up on baseball and turned his attention towards cleaning up the environment. The last anyone heard, he was working on a machine that would compress the wind around Winslow and convert it into a manageable force that could be used to blow the polluted air from big city skies.

Perhaps Junior's marvelous experiment with the elements will bring him greater success, not to mention the chance to rid Winslow of some excess wind.

CHAPTER 8

Pert was a Purty Good Cottonpicker

A large number of early settlers came to Arizona, not in search of gold or fertile fields to plow, but because of their health. The dry climate could cure everything except lovesickness.

Minnie Elliott came to Scottsdale around 1900 suffering from tuberculosis. She became friendly with the local Pima Indians and they insisted on curing her. Each day they took the frail woman out and buried her up to her neck in the warm desert sand. They also concocted a bitter tea for her made from the creosote bush. Fortunately, no tourist happened by and saw the natives treating poor Minnie because it looked like she was undergoing some horrible torture and Arizona's reputation as a wild and woolly place was already bad enough as it was. Minnie was cured eventually and lived to a ripe old age.

Rosa Edwards was the belle of San Antonio, Texas, around the turn of the century. She married Wesley Walker Trimble and the two eventually settled at Langtry, Texas, on the Rio Grande. A few years later, she came down with asthma and shriveled up to a tiny thing of less than eighty pounds. The doctors told her she had only a few weeks to live unless she left Texas and headed for some dry place like Arizona.

When they arrived at the railroad station in Tempe, Arizona in 1917, she was so weak she had to be carried off the train. But the hot, dry climate quickly restored her health and within a few weeks she hired out picking cotton in Scottsdale. Pretty soon she was known far and wide as the cotton pickin' best in the Salt River Valley. She'd drag one of those long tow sacks up and down the row with three kids playing on it.

She was a wiry lady with quick hands and, because of her boundless energy, folks called her Pert, a name she kept the rest of her life. Pert filled those cotton sacks up so fast that they finally gave her a whole cotton field to pick all by herself. One time they raced her against one of those newfangled mechanical cotton picking machines and Pert wore the dern thing out. The owners of the machine were so humiliated they sold it to the state fairgrounds to use for making cotton candy at fairs.

One day Pert learned that her sister, Sadie, back in Texas, was on her deathbed suffering from asthma. She rushed down to the station, but was told the next train wouldn't leave until the following day. So, she borrowed a bicycle, and started peddling for Texas as fast as she could.

Pert arrived in San Antonio early the next day and went directly to the hospital. She was shocked to see her poor sister looking so pale and wan. She knew immediately only one thing could save poor Sadie: some of that healthy Arizona air. Pert rushed downstairs, picked up her bike, and hauled it up to Sadie's room. She held one of the tires right under Sadie's nose and pressed on the valve core. As that pure, dry air filled her nostrils, Sadie's color returned and her eyes snapped open.

"We've got to hurry," Pert warned, "I've barely got enough breathing air in these two tires to get us back to Arizona."

On the way out of the hospital, Sadie, now frisky as a spring colt, slowed down just long enough to pinch a male doctor on the derriere.

Pert and Sadie got on that bicycle and started peddling back to Arizona, stopping every so often to let a little air out of the tires and get rejuvenated. By the time they reached El Paso, Pert was beginning to tire, she always was a frail woman, so Sadie took over the peddling and finished the trip with Pert sitting on the handlebars.

Neither of those Texas ladies ever had any desire to go back East (to Texas) and breathe that unhealthy air again.

As Arizona became more crowded, the air around Phoenix wasn't as pure anymore, so they moved to Ajo where they lived in good health for the next seventy-five years or so.

GRAHAM

CHAPTER 9

Practicin' Medicine

The frontier was a great place for a doctor to practice, and that's exactly what many of them needed . . . practice. A great deal of experimental surgery took place as doctors didn't have to perform under the same restraints as their colleagues in the more established East. Doctor George Goodfellow of Tombstone, for example, performed the first perineal prostatectomy in medical history. He also became a foremost authority on the treatment of gunshot wounds. That's not surprising when considering his boisterous clientele.

Some physicians came to Arizona from back East because their practice had failed for one reason or another. A few were incompetent, others had drinking problems. Since doctors were scarce out West, folks tended to overlook their shortcomings. A doctor once told his patient, "I can't find any cause for your illness. I suspect it's because of drinking."

"That's OK doc," said the patient, "I'll come back when you're sober!"

Old Doc Starley of Chino Valley got an excited call late one night from a cowhand named Cal Pyle up near Hell Canyon. "Doc, doc, it's my Sadie! She's startin' them labor pains, jest like you said!"

"Now calm down, Cal. Get yourself together."

"OK doc, but what shall I do?"

"First," the doctor said, "tell me, how far apart are the pains coming?"

"Why doc, uh—they're all in the same place!"

"The best way to keep from getting constipation," Doc Starley told Sherman Dubbs, "is to drink warm water an hour before dinner every night."

A few weeks later Doc Starley ran into Sherman in Prescott and asked him how he was feeling.

"Terrible." Sherman replied.

"Did you drink warm water an hour before dinner each night like I told you?"

"I tried doc, but who can keep drinking for more than ten minutes at a time?"

Occasionally a doctor would let personal feelings affect his professional practice. Sometimes that seemingly worked for the benefit of the patient. At the famous "Six-gun Classic" at Florence in 1888, Joe Phy and Pete

Gabriel, personal and political enemies of longstanding, opened fire on each other in a local saloon. When the smoke cleared, Phy had three bullets in his body. He was quickly treated by his friend, Dr. Bill Harvey. Gabriel had two serious wounds, one in the groin, and one in the chest. Dr. Harvey refused to treat Gabriel, whom he didn't like. Gabriel survived anyway while Dr. Harvey's patient, Joe Phy died.

Ranch women could be as roughshod and unwashed as the men. One time, Sadie Johnson, a big, rawboned woman rancher who always dressed in men's clothes and boots came into Dr. Ben N. Payne's office complaining of a sore ankle. She pulled off her boot and exposed a horny foot.

"Madam," he said, holding his nose, "that is the dirtiest damn foot in Arizona."

"I'll bet you five bucks it ain't," she cheerfully retorted.

The bet was made and with a roar of laughter, she removed the other boot and exclaimed with great aplomb, "That one is!"

Doc Payne agreed and paid off the wager.

Ol' Rooster Hopgood paid a visit to Doc Payne one time complaining of a pain in his knee. "Why, that's just old age!" the doc explained.

"But Doc," Rooster complained, "my other knee's just as old and it don't hurt a bit!"

Ol' Doc Payne had to have quite a sense of humor to put up with that kind of nonsense. But he could hand it out, too! One day, he hung a sign in his window advertising brain transplants. He claimed if you wanted a brain from a lawyer, it would cost you $100,000. A doctor's brain would set you back $200,000. But the most expensive was the brain of a cowboy. It cost $300,000.

"Why is the cowboy's brain more expensive?" came the inevitable inquiry.

"Because it's never been used!" was Doc's dead-panned reply.

Buck Fancher was a fiesty old cowpuncher who'd never seen the inside of a hospital until he was nearly seventy years old. He didn't fancy being cooped up in a hospital bed and didn't care much for the grub they served—especially since it was being fed through a tube into his rectum. For an old puncher who'd lived on beans, beef, and black coffee most of his life, this was the ultimate indignity. He wanted a beefsteak in the worst way and tried to bribe the head nurse to sneak one to him. She looked him square in the eye and replied haughtily, "You're getting enough nourishment by means of rectal feeding." He pleaded with the doctor and got a similar response.

The next morning, when the head nurse made her rounds, Buck gave her a friendly smile and said invitingly, "Would you and the doctor be kind enough to drop in at noon today. And bring along a couple of extra tubes. I'd like for you to join me for lunch!"

Doc Cartwright knocked on the cubicle door before entering. "Come on in," Grandma Slade called out. Doc had Grandma remove all her clothing and then examined her all over—from top to bottom and front to back.

Afterwards, she said, "Doc, can I ask you a question?"

"Of course," he grunted.

"Why did you bother to knock?"

Pain was common on the frontier. Old battle wounds, horse accidents, guns, wagons, and mines all contributed. Morphine, opium, and laudanum were the most popular painkillers of the times and were easily accessible. Hypodermic needles weren't available so doctors rubbed opium or morphine into a cut to relax the patient.

Trapper John Smith found himself in the wilderness with a severe toothache, hundreds of miles from a dentist. In desperation, he swapped all his furs at a trading post for a bottle of laudanum to kill the pain until he could get to a doctor. Along the way he was jumped by a war party of Indians, who came into his camp and took what remained of John's possessions.

Trapper John was so high on the opium derivative that he didn't seem to mind the intrusion. Their curiosity aroused, the braves took his bottle and sampled its contents and immediately went down for the count on the strong substance. Trapper John then casually broke up their weapons, stampeded their ponies, retrieved his goods, and continued his trek to the doctor.

Do-it-yourself medicines were of the rough and ready kind. Whiskey was the king of remedies. It was used to cure everything from colds and rheumatism to arthritis and boredom. It was also an antiseptic.

Ol' John Barleycorn was also the cause of many medical emergencies. Some of that liquor was strong enough to peel the hide off a Gila monster. One crusty doctor opined, after treating a bunch of hell-raising cowboys, "If they can get drunk and shoot up one another, they can be sewed up without drugs."

Some practitioners prescribed mild amounts of alcohol to their patients before bedtime. The thought being the medicinal effects might not be much but the patients went to sleep relaxed and happy. Alcohol was especially popular among little old ladies and church deacons who wouldn't otherwise dare touch a drop of "Ol' Redeye." Patent medicine salesmen sold products with a high alcoholic content. Customers seldom complained.

Grannies were the fountainhead of medicine on the frontier. Granny's reputation grew with each new cure she affected. Sometimes the patient would have gotten well without any treatment at all. Other times there was true medicinal value in granny medicine. Still others got well in spite of Granny's remedy. In all cases, Granny usually got full credit for the cure. Granny medicine operated on the voodoo premise—the fiercer the ailment, the more drastic the cure. Any child who was ever force-fed castor oil can attest to that.

Granny cured baldness by mixing a quart of clean tar, a quart of whiskey, and a quart of honey or molasses in a pewter dish which was then heated to a near boil. Skim off the tar and then bottle the rest. Take a tablespoon five times a day and hair would grow again. Bad breath was cured by washing one's mouth in one's own urine. To induce labor, Granny stuffed a pinch of snuff up the patient's nose to make her sneeze.

Blood was purified with sulfur and molasses. Whooping cough was cured by having the child cough on a live fish, then releasing the fish and observe. If the fish came out of the water to cough, it was a sign the fish had caught it and the child would get well. Warts were cured by spitting on them and letting a horse kick the afflicted area.

Most of the saddleback practitioners on the frontier were bona fide, however, many others were merely wannabes. Since licenses weren't required until late in the 19th century, many simply hung out a shingle and went into the business of healing folks. They usually stayed around as long as they didn't do something catastrophic to their patients.

Richard Carter was a self-proclaimed doctor who ran a successful practice for a number of years then wrote a book about it. He told of one occasion when he was feeling poorly and set aside a sample of his own urine to settle.

He left the room and while he was away, a female patient taking a pregnancy test came in, poured out the contents of the glass and filled it with her own specimen. She failed to tell him what she'd done and when he made a lab test, discovered he was pregnant. Knowing he was physically unable to deliver, he claimed he was planning to give himself an abortion when the mixup was discovered.

One of Doc Carter's most memorable cases was the treating of a hypochondriac named George Sweeny. Sweeny swore he had a bellyful of ducks. He could even hear them quacking deep inside his abdominal area. So Doc prescribed a purge. As the purge was doing its work, Doc miraculously popped a brace of quacking ducklings into the washbasin.

The patient was duly impressed and wanted to know how the ducks got into his belly in the first place. Doc asked if eggs were a part of his daily diet. When the patient replied in the affirmative, Doc replied matter-of-factly that he must have eaten some duck eggs by mistake and a few had hatched. The patient, Doc reported, swore off eggs from that time on. Coincidentally, the quacking in his belly ceased. Locals proudly proclaimed Doc Carter the town's "Official Quack Doctor."

CHAPTER 10

You Can Lead a Man to Politics . . . but You Can't Make Him Think

Ialways wanted to be so indefinite enough about every-thing that someday they'd make me a politician and that finally happened in 1987. A group of college students were unhappy with the political situation in Arizona so they snatched my hat and threw it in the ring as a Republican candidate for governor. I tried to retrieve it, but by the time I did, they were wearing T-shirts printed with "Marshall Trimble for Governor" on the front. Politics is kinda like sex—you don't have to be good at it to enjoy it. Needless to say, the call to serve overwhelmed me. Besides, I'd do anything for money except work, so politics seemed like a good career choice.

We decided my campaign slogan should be something inspiring and thoughtful, yet contain substance, so we finally settled on: "My Limitations are Limitless." Like any political campaigner, I sought to give the Arizonans things they wanted to hear, so my first campaign promise was to make it rain more often. A few thought that idea was all wet, but I did manage to place most of the blame on our dry weather on California. Next, I promised the folks out in the desert at Gila Bend that every other summer I'd let them trade places with the citizens in the cool mountain town of Alpine. Incidentally, that one didn't play well in Alpine.

Overcrowding in the state is becoming a major problem. When one of my researchers noted that every ninety-six minutes some woman in the state gives birth, I immediately declared that we should find her and make her stop.

A plan for cleaning up the air is important for every aspiring politician, so I proposed to make the legislature meet outdoors. All that hot air would lift the pollution into the higher elevations above Phoenix and the accompanying wind would carry it beyond the borders of Arizona.

My economic advice to consumers was to live within your means—even if you had to borrow to do so!

On educational matters, I would require that universities plan their programs with an end in view—not to mention a few guards, tackles, and a couple of hard-throwing quarterbacks.

Well, by this time, the media was beginning to take notice of the campaign, proving that a creative, grassroots campaign can still find success in American politics. I was asked to appear on some radio talk shows in Phoenix. One host asked what I'd do about traffic problems in Phoenix. By this time, I was so driven (no pun intended) and inspired that ideas just popped into my head and there was nothing there to stop them. "Traffic has gotten so bad," I declared, "that if you wanted to hit a pedestrian you had to get out of your car to do it." I proposed that people not be allowed to drive their cars until they were paid for. (I borrowed most of those time-less tidbits of political wisdom from my idol, Will Rogers.)

One talk show host said I needed only one kicker to put me over the hump so I proposed that we annex San Diego. Arizona needs and richly deserves some ocean-front property and California has more than it needs. My plan was a surefire winner. Keeping in mind, that each August, some four million Arizonans vacation in San Diego, I would select a date—say August 15—and ask everyone to secretly enter the city and act like nothing is out of the ordinary. Just go to the beach and have fun. Then, on the 15th, four million Arizonans would rise in unison and declare San Diego a part of our state. Who could stop us? Well, the switchboard lit up like a Christmas tree. People were calling in wanting to support me for governor. Inspired by the idea of gaining a seacoast for the state, many wanted to launch an attack immediately. There are some interesting folks out there in talk radio land!

Like any good politician, I figured we should lower taxes and do away with income taxes. As most folks know, income tax has made more liars out of Americans than fishing and golf combined. I promised to get taxes down low enough that citizens could afford to pay them. Taxes got me in more trouble than any other issue. It happened during a political speech when someone in the back of a noisy crowd asked what I thought of taxes.

I didn't hear clearly and responded by saying, "I love Texas!" And I do! But the media picked up on that and the next day's headlines read, "Trimble Loves Taxes." Well, that about did me in. It's hard to escape those kinds of public perceptions.

During the sizzling summer of 1987, my campaign was sustained on a lot of hot air, most of it provided by me. During one enthusiastic campaign speech, I righteously declared, "I'd be the best dern governor money could buy!" The media jumped all over me for that one, too!

By fall, when things started cooling off, my enthusiasm began to evaporate. It was lots of fun until we began to believe I might actually win, and then what would we do?

Luckily, I encountered only one heckler during the campaign, but he was a real pistol. It happened one summer afternoon in Globe. This fella kept on interrupting me, so I finally stopped and asked what was his problem? He righteously declared, "My grandfather was a Democrat, my father was a Democrat, and, by God, I am a Democrat!"

I looked at him and wondered aloud, "Well then, if your grandfather was a jackass, and your father was a jackass, what does that make you?"

"A Republican!" he replied.

He had me there.

CHAPTER 11

Don't Make Any Treaties with These Guys and Other Navajo Sage Tales

Concho Slade was doing some horse trading at Teec Nos Pos, on the Navajo Reservation, several years ago and, since it was getting late in the day, he accepted an invitation to spend the night at his old friend Hosteen Many Goats' hogan. That evening, he rode over to Many Goats', got down off his horse, and tied him to the hitching rail. While they were rolling smokes and discussing the various virtues and vices of horses they'd known, Hosteen's wife untied Concho's bedroll and tossed it inside the hogan. Then she unsaddled his horse and threw the saddle, blankets, and bridle over the hitching rail.

Concho observed the proceedings uneasily, wondering to himself if it would be safe to leave his gear outside overnight. The old Navajo sensed his apprehension, "You don't have to worry about your outfit, Concho," he said reassuringly, "there isn't a white man within two day's ride of here."

Shine Smith was a zealous Presbyterian missionary to the Navajo during the 1930s; that is, until the church leaders relieved him of his duties. He refused to leave and continued to preach his patented hellfire and damnation. His Navajo congregation always listened to Shine's sermons with courteous respect. They were particularly curious about one sermon where he told the miracle story of Jesus walking on water. "Jesus was able to perform such a miracle because he had faith," Shine declared with conviction.

A few days after the "walk-on-water" sermon, Shine was trying to cross the Little Colorado River in his old Model T Ford up near the trading post at Cameron. About halfway across, the tin lizzie sank up to its axle in quicksand.

Several Navajo observed Shine's dilemma from the bank with mild curiosity. As the horseless carriage sank deeper in the muddy-colored water, he hollered over to them to help pull him out. They grinned and waved back, but otherwise ignored his pleas. Finally, someone rode over and told the post trader. He got a long rope and pulled the preacher and his Model T out.

"Why didn't you fellas help ol' Shine?" the trader asked afterward.

They glanced at one another, then one shrugged his shoulders and replied, "We were waiting to witness a miracle."

During recent years, the Navajo people have become a powerful force in Arizona politics. Politicians campaigning for office spend a great deal of time traveling across the vast reservation, visiting chapter houses and making speeches, courting the Navajo voters. Not long ago, a politician from Phoenix decided he'd fit in better among the Navajo if he looked more like a cowboy.

He visited a local Western clothing store and bought a pair of cowboy boots, hat, shirt, and levis thinking those duds would make him seem like a real man of the soil. In reality, he looked more like he'd just stepped out of a Shepler's catalog. As he approached the chapter house at Greasewood, a group of curious folks gathered around to hear what he had to say.

The politician introduced himself and made a few remarks about how he wished he could live out in the great outdoors.

"Dola be chaa," one of the spectators replied, smiling broadly. The others nodded in agreement.

Now that kind of friendly response is enough to encourage any politician to keep spreading it on.

"If you vote for me, I promise to let you live in your traditional way for as long as the grass shall grow," he continued.

This time several others joined in with a resounding, "Dola be chaa."

Thus reassured, the politician stepped up the oratory. "I will bring more industry to Navajoland, and, furthermore, I promise to provide jobs for everyone."

This time everyone in the crowd chorused, "Dola be chaa."

The politician smiled back at the gathering and raised his arms in triumph. Being astute about such things, he figured he'd quit while he was ahead. He said his good-bys, shook hands all around, then headed for his car, which was on the opposite side of a large cowpen. Part way around he decided to take a shortcut through the corral. As he started to crawl through the rail, one of his hosts grinned and cautioned, "Be careful not to step in any Dola be chaa."

An old Hopi artist was leaning against a wall at the Museum of Northern Arizona during a fair a few years ago when an Eastern lady walked up and asked him to explain how he knew when to go up to the Hopi mesas for a ceremony. Very slowly and with a great deal of sign language she asked, "Do you know by phases of the moon, or do you read something in the stars?"

"Neither," he replied slowly, "I just get on the telephone and call the Hopi Cultural Center and they tell me!"

An old Hopi artist was leaning against a wall at the

Back in 1862, a company of U.S. troops was cautiously approaching Apache Pass. Deep inside the treacherous canyon came the ominous sound of Apache drums. Major Catastrophe turned to his commander, General Confusion and said grimly, "General, I don't like the sound of those drums!"

"I don't either," the General replied.

A voice called out from deep within the pass, "He's not our regular drummer!"

Yazzie Begay stopped in at the blood bank in Flagstaff to make a donation. Afterwards, the attendant, a young lady recently arrived from the East, asked politely, "Are you a full-blooded Indian?"

"Not anymore," Yazzie said straight-faced, "now I'm a pint short!"

Another time, Yazzie walked into Babbitt's building material store in Flagstaff and told the clerk he wanted to buy some two-by-fours.

"How long do you want them?" the clerk asked.

"For a long, long time," came Yazzie's puzzled reply. "I'm planning to build a corral with them."

Since a good part of the Colorado Plateau in northern Arizona bears a resemblance to moonscape, it was a natural place for NASA to train the astronauts for the landing on the moon. One day, while they were out practicing their maneuvers, an old Navajo medicine man watched curiously from a nearby hill. Finally, he ambled down and approached a well-dressed and urbane-looking Navajo wearing a grey Brooks Brothers suit who was from tribal headquarters and wanted to know what was going on.

The old man didn't speak English, so the conversation took place in Navajo. Grey-Suit Navajo pointed out that these men were training to make a journey into space. "They will be the first people from earth," he explained patiently, "to set foot on the moon."

The medicine man shook his head. "That's not so," he corrected. "A long time ago some of Our People left the earth on a journey to the sun and, on their journey, stopped at the moon."

When Grey-Suit translated what the old man had said, NASA decided this would make a great media event, adding a new dimension to the voyage. So they asked Grey-Suit if they could get the old man to agree to speak into a tape recorder and give a message for the astronauts to take along and pass on to any Navajo who might still be on the moon.

Grey-Suit explained NASA's request to the old man and asked if he had any words of wisdom he'd like to pass along to his brothers on the moon. The old man agreed and, without hesitation, spoke a few words in his native language into the recorder. Afterwards, the folks at NASA could hardly contain their curiosity. "What words of wisdom," they asked anxiously, "did he offer to his brothers on the moon?"

"Don't make any treaties with these guys!" was the straight-faced response.

CHAPTER 12

Ol' Tom Edison &
the Hopi

Famous creative people and inventors have been long associated with Arizona. Local legend claims George Westinghouse lived in the mining town of Duquesne. Frank Lloyd Wright spent a lot of time around Scottsdale and Sam Colt invested in an early mining venture south of Tucson. Few people realize that perhaps the most famous American inventor, Thomas Edison, also had a close association with Arizona.

Back East, folks greeted his newly invented incandescent light bulb with suspicion. They'd been using kerosene lamps and were reluctant to make such a universal change. Besides, electricity was a mysterious and dangerous force that was looked upon with apprehension and fear. For a time, it looked like the electric light bulb was doomed to failure.

This revolutionary invention of light was saved by the vision of the most traditional people in America—the Hopi Indians. The ancient Hopi city of Walpi sits atop a narrow, steep-sided mesa. Outhouses for the residents were perched precariously on the edge of the mesa, several hundred feet above the valley floor.

The Hopi elders recognized the dangers for residents walking to and fro from the privies after dark and believed Tom Edison's new light bulb might solve their dilemma. They contacted the discouraged inventor and invited him out to Walpi for a demonstration. Edison quickly saw this as an opportunity to show the world how his light bulb worked. So, a deal was struck and Tom Edison eventually placed electric lights in all of the outhouses on the Hopi mesas. And, as they say, the rest is history.

Tom Edison was a pioneer innovator in the first degree, but his proudest achievement was that of being the first to wire a head for a reservation.

CHAPTER 13

Small Town, Arizona

Over the past fifty years or so, I've lived in a scattering of Arizona towns. I was born in Mesa, but we lived in Tempe at the time. Actually, we lived in Kyrene. Later, we resided in Mesa, Lehi, Scottsdale, Glendale, and several parts of Phoenix. I have the unique distinction of being claimed by four towns: Mesa claims I'm from Tempe, Tempe claims I'm from Scottsdale, Scottsdale claims I'm from Glendale, and Glendale claims I'm from Phoenix.

I spent my formative years in the small northern Arizona town of Ashfork. How small was it? Ashfork was so small we had to share our one horse with another town. The "Entering Town" and "Leaving Town" signs were hung on the same fencepost. The town was so small that one year, when we held a St. Patrick's Day parade, the only participants were me, a fellow that owned an Irish Setter, and another guy who owned a record album by the Clancy Brothers and Tommy Makem. When the highway department painted a white line down the middle of

Main Street, they had to widen the street. Ashfork wasn't exactly the end of the world, but they used to say you could stand on your tiptoes and see the end of the world from there.

Even though we were on "America's Main Street"— Route 66—very few people stopped longer than to eat and buy gas. The only tourists who stayed over were Oklahomans on their way to Bakersfield who'd broken down or run out of gas. The only foreigners we ever met were Californians. I've lost count of the number of people who've said to me: "I spent two weeks in Ashfork one afternoon!" Consuelo Corona used to say that if she only had two weeks to live, she'd like to live them in Ashfork . . . because two weeks there would seem like a lifetime!"

The town had no water, so each day the Santa Fe Railroad hauled water in from Chino Valley. One time the local water company got into a conservation mood and asked the citizens to only flush their toilets once a week. That created quite a stink among the citizens. Another time a tourist noticed a rancher loading up his pickup with fifty gallon barrels of water.

"Where ya takin' the water?" he asked curiously. "To my ranch," the man replied.

"How far away is your ranch?" he asked. "Five miles north of here."

"Wouldn't it be easier to drill a well at your ranch?"

"Nope, same distance to water either way—five miles!"

Ashfork also holds the dubious record for longevity of wind and blowing dust. It started in 1882 when the town was founded and hasn't quit yet. Winslow likes to claim the record, but it's on good authority that it did stop blowing once and a whole herd of cattle fell over. When locals wanted to know which way the wind was blowing, they just looked out their windows to see which way the water tower was leaning.

When the town was founded over a century ago, it was located just sixteen miles east of Kingman. At last count, Ashfork is now over a hundred miles further east.

Harvey Culpepper went in to see the banker about a loan on his ranch. The banker says, "Before I can loan you the money, I need to go out and see your ranch." "Ain't necessary," Harvey says, looking out the window. "Here she comes now!"

Ashfork was a nice place to live but you wouldn't want to visit. Small towns do have endearing characteristics. You know you're in a small town when you call a wrong telephone number and wind up talking for thirty minutes anyway. Or, when you move across town and don't have to leave a forwarding address with the postman. A small town is where everybody knows who the father of the pups is and everybody knows whosd checks are good and whose husbands aren't.

Ashfork was an outlying community. We could outlie anybody. The residents were a collection of self-reliant and independent folks who were suspicious of any outsider, especially someone from a city. Jake Smelser had a sign in his front yard that said "Firewood For Sale." One day a city slicker drove up and asked Jake if he took orders for firewood. Jake looked him straight in the eye and replied, "Mister, I cut firewood, I haul firewood, and I sell firewood. But I don't take orders from nobody!"

One day, not long ago, Amos Slocum was sitting on a bench outside Freddie's Texaco station whittling on a stick. Next to him, a mangy black dog was basking in the sun. While waiting for his car to get gassed, a tourist from California decided to acquaint himself with the locals. He walked over hoping to make friends with the dog. As he approached, the dog bared its teeth and growled. The Californian backed off and asked Amos, "Does your dog bite?"

"Nope." Amos replied.

The tourist smiled and relaxed. He reached out a hand and the potlicker promptly jumped up and bit him.

"I thought you said your dog doesn't bite," the Californian whimpered.

"That ain't *my* dog!" Amos muttered.

Ashfork's illustrious citizens weren't considered suave or debonaire by some standards but, when given a chance, they could be just as uptown as the next place, especially when it came to the latest in home decorating trends. When the new Wal-Mart opened in Prescott a few years ago, a bunch of folks drove down and bought some of that newfangled indoor-outdoor carpet and installed it in their outdoor privies.

The nicest restaurant in town was the Arizona Cafe, owned by Harold and Sadie Ruppert. They were a perfect pair; he was paunchy and she was punchy! Harold's only qualification as a gourmet was that he'd been a cook on a Navy destroyer. The specialty of the house was "Gourmet Roadkill" and nobody could fix it quite like Harold.

Next door was the Arizona Bar. The regulars were a mixture of cowboys, railroaders, and miners. The latter were also known affectionately as "rock doodlers." It was a very democratic bar, especially on Saturday night. Everybody was welcome except preachers and pacifists.

The Arizona Bar was also the second office of Dr. Rufus Cartwright, the town doctor. He was an elderly gent who always wore a long black coat and black hat pulled down over his eyes. Doc was also the town magician—he could walk down the street and turn into a saloon. Doc never made any money practicing medicine, he couldn't make both ends meet because he was too busy making one end drink.

Doc's regular office was at the Harvey House, but he met most of his customers at the Arizona Bar. You never had to sit for a long spell in a waiting room, just go to the back booth and wake up Doc Cartwright. One day after examining a patient, Doc said, "I can't find the problem . . . I suspect it's because of drinking."

The patient smiled cheerfully and replied, "That's OK Doc, I'll come back when you're sober!"

Doc always carried a pocketful of pills and when someone needed a prescription filled, he'd just reach into a pocket and pull out a handful. One time Doc gave an old cowboy some pills and advised him to take a pill for two days, then skip the third day. Four days later, the cowboy came into the Arizona Bar looking pale and wan. He went back to Doc's booth, "I'm plum worn out, Doc," he complained, "I took the pills OK, but skippin' that third day dang near killed me!"

Across the street from the Arizona Bar was the five and dime store, owned by Jacob Solomon, who also served as the justice of peace. The location made it convenient for the local deputy to haul the unruly drunks up for a hearing. During the election of 1948, the county registrar of voters in Prescott called the judge and wanted to know the number of voters in Ashfork broken down by sex. Judge Solomon replied straight-faced, "None that I know of, our main problem is alcohol!"

In 1950, the census taker called on Henrietta Koontz and asked her how many children she had.

"Well," she said, "there was the first set of twins, Lulu and Lola, then there was the second set of twins Willie and Joe, and then there was the third set of twins, Pat and Mike . . ."

At this point the census taker interrupted and asked, "Did you always get twins?"

"Gosh no!" she explained, "we done it thousands of other times and got nothing at all."

Town socialite, Rowena Twitty and her husband Chester, were inseparable—and it usually took several policemen to pull them apart. Rowena was about to have a birthday and Chester was at his wits end trying to think of a gift for the occasion. When he asked what she wanted she just replied, "I really don't think I should say."

"How about a diamond necklace?" "No, I don't want a necklace," she declared.

"Then how about a mink coat?" "No, I don't like furs."

She even declined his offer of a new car. Finally, Chester threw his hands up in despair. "Well, Rowena, just what *do* you want?"

"A divorce," she shouted. "That's what I really want!"

Chester thought about that for a moment and replied, "Well, I wasn't planning on spending quite *that* much!"

A fella in Ashfork I used to know, Pinky Graveldinger, was deaf as a hitching post and for years all his friends and relatives had been urging him to get a hearing aid. "I ain't hard of hearin'," he insisted, "folks jest ain't talkin' loud enough."

Then one day Pinky saw a sign in Judge Solomon's hardware store advertising a 60% off sale on hearing aids. He hurried inside and, within a few minutes, was fitted with a new hearing aid. He stepped out on the street wearing a broad grin. The first person he met was Stump Rollins who pointed at Pinky's ear and said, "Graveldinger, what's that thing in your ear?"

"This," Pinky proudly proclaimed, "is my new state-of-the-art hearing aid. Everybody was right. It's wonderful! Now I can hear like a kid again!"

"That's great!" said Stump. "What kind is it?"

Pinky pulled out his pocket watch and exclaimed, "A quarter to five!"

Old Tommy Nunez was the town barber. It was claimed that when he moved to Ashfork, the San Francisco Peaks was just a prairie dog town. He was so old his toupee had turned grey. A reporter once asked Tony that wearing question, "To what do you attribute your old age?"

Tommy replied matter-of-factly, "To the fact that I was born a very long time ago!"

Tommy the barber was also one of the most pessimistic guys you ever met. No matter what kind of good news you had, Tommy would find some way to put a damper on it. One time Claude Pew was sitting in the barber chair getting a haircut. He was all excited about a trip he was taking to the state fair at Phoenix.

Tommy just looked at him and said, "Claude, why do you want to go to Phoenix? It's crowded and the traffic is terrible. You won't like it."

"I'll get to see the governor," Claude explained.

"Let me tell you something about that," Tommy said authoritatively.

"He'll be way up on that platform, surrounded by security guards, and you'll be just another face in the crowd. He won't even know you're there. That's as close as you're going to get to seeing the governor!"

Claude went on his trip anyway and when he came back, Tommy asked, "Well, Claude, how was Phoenix?"

"You were right about Phoenix. It's crowded and the traffic is terrible."

"What'd I tell ya," Tommy laughed, "and did you get to see the governor?"

"Yeah, but you were only half right about that," Claude explained. "He was up on that platform and I was standing out there among hundreds of people, but then two men wearing dark suits came up to me and said the governor wanted to see me. And they took me right up there on the platform with him."

"What did he tell you," Tommy asked, his curiosity aroused.

"He didn't tell me anything."

"Well, what did he ask you?" Tommy inquired impatiently.

"He just wanted to know where I got this god-awful haircut."

Because of the transient nature of the populace, crime was always a problem. Any cat with a tail was considered a tourist. They used to say you could walk a block in any direction and never leave the scene of a crime. Our high school principal used to stand outside the gate of the schoolhouse each morning and search everybody for guns and, if you didn't have one, he'd give you one.

The Great Depression was still going on in Ashfork in the 1940s. We were poor but didn't know it. Oklahomans on their way to California to escape the dust bowl felt sorry for us and gave us chickens from the coops atop their old cars. One Christmas we received Care packages from Ethiopia.

The town couldn't afford a radar gun so sheriff's deputy, Hector Pacheco, had to use his wife's hair dryer. He could sure make those Californians put on the skids.

When you're raised in a town like Ashfork, you get used to other towns poking fun at you. Even the radio stations in Phoenix got into the act. One station used to announce: "It's ten o'clock in Phoenix. Do you know where your children are?" They'd follow that with, "It's ten o'clock in Prescott. Do you know where your husband is?" The third one was the kicker. They'd say, "It's ten o'clock in Ashfork. Do you know what time it is?"

In the early 1950s, I considered myself a whoopswagger hellraiser. Probably the wildest stunt I ever got mixed up in was the time Louie Quackenbush stole a can of beer from his old man's icebox and nine of us got roaring drunk on it. We were out in the barn and decided to roll our own cigarettes with toilet paper and cow manure. That was the first and last time I ever tried smoking.

During the summer of 1954, Becky Delgado moved in across the street from me. She was very pretty and the object of my unsophisticated amorous pursuits. Too shy for a frontal approach, I flirted with her from a distance. Whenever she would go into the privy behind her house I'd try to get her attention by bombarding it with rocks. Needless to say, that wrecked any chance for a meaningful relationship. She left Ashfork at the end of that summer and I didn't see her again. I heard later she became a Playboy bunny. I knew then I'd better learn some smoother techniques.

My worldly knowledge up to then was bound by Kingman on the west and Holbrook on the east. Since the town had no television and radio reception was poor, most of my knowledge of the outside work was learned while pumping gas at the local gas station to tourists traveling along Route 66.

I was then, and continue to be, fascinated by trains, especially those old-time cabooses. We used to jump the freights and ride up the hill eighteen miles to Williams. One time the bulls caught us and hauled us in. They'd take your name and, if your dad worked for Santa Fe, he'd be in big trouble with the officials. So I picked an elderly bachelor hoghead named Frenchy Nichols and claimed he was my old man.

I was sixteen years old in 1955. By then the railroad was about to quit the town and old Route 66 was getting ready to bypass Ashfork. My parents moved away. I found them three years later, living in Phoenix under assumed names.

CHAPTER 14

Short Tales

Tucson considers itself the "Mother of Cities" in Arizona, and for good reason. The community was founded in 1775, long before there were any non-Indian settlements north of the Gila River. When Arizona was a U.S. Territory, Tucson was a perennial candidate for the capital until a young upstart named Phoenix claimed it for good in 1889. It was Arizona's largest city until Phoenix claimed that honor in 1920. A few Tucsonans, chagrined that Phoenix continues to grab an unfair share of the spotlight, have even proposed that southern Arizona secede and form a new state.

This deep-seated rivalry crops up in other unexpected places. Recently, I was headed into the rugged Galiuro Mountains and stopped in Tucson to buy a small pocket compass. I tried several places without having any luck. Finally, I explained my dilemma to a clerk in a large outdoor equipment store.

"I don't think you'll have any luck finding one in Tucson," he explained. "We don't have any use here for some little gadget that don't do nothin' but point to Phoenix!"

Then there was the time a Phoenix TV reporter was needling the mayor of Tucson by pointing out that hundreds of Tucsonans had migrated to Phoenix during the past decade.

"Mayor," the interviewer droned on, "can you tell us how you feel about so many native Tucsonans leaving for a better life in Phoenix?"

The mayor merely smiled and replied, "I believe it raises the level of intelligence in both communities."

Two rather well-dressed women were seen recently chatting poolside at a posh Paradise Valley resort. One was obviously showing the other the sights. She pointed out the pool and tennis courts, noting they were not only for guests but, for a small fee, anyone could use the facilities.

"But how do you keep out the riffraff," her friend wanted to know.

"No problem," she replied, "in Paradise Valley, the riffraff have their own pools and tennis courts."

While visiting San Antonio, this Yankee from Boston asked a native, "Say, what's that old rundown looking building over there?"

"Why suh," the Texan proudly replied, "that is the Alamo, a mighty sacred place. In that building, 186 brave Texans held off Santy Anna's army of 12,000 for thirteen days!"

"Um-m-m," said the Easterner, "and who is that statue supposed to represent?"

"Why that, suh, is a Texas Ranger. He once fought off 2,000 Comanches armed with just a six-shooter!"

"My good man," the Bostonian smiled, "where I come from, we have heroes, too. For instance, there was Paul Revere . . ."

"Paul Revere," snorted the Texan, "wasn't he the fella who had to *ride* for help?"

Voting irregularities in the Arizona territory were as common sunshine. In an 1870 election in Yuma County, Yuma Indians lined up in droves wearing breechclouts and stovepipe hats. When the clerk asked their names, the natives grinned and replied in mock innocence, "O'Toole, Murphy, or Sullivan." It was usually, "vote early and often!"

There was a heated discussion following the election, and the group was evenly divided as to their honesty until candidate Elwood Pringle stepped forward and said, "I know the elections are crooked. I voted for myself three times, but when the returns were completed, I never got a single vote!"

Back in the 1890s, Republicans were few and far between in Arizona. Arizonans were pretty upset with the Republicans in Washington who were responsible for closing down the silver mines and putting lots of people out of work. Old-timers said a man claiming to be a Republican was either a newcomer or a damn fool. After an election in Globe, officials were tabulating the ballots were surprised to find a Republican vote. No one seemed to know what to do, so the sheriff said, "Let's hold it out until the final tally." Surprisingly, another Republican vote turned up. "That settles it," the sheriff declared, "that rotten scalawag voted twice, so we won't count either of 'em!"

An old cowman, Rance Marley, a staunch believer in psychology and high morale, called his hands together one day and said, "Boys, in running this outfit, I want you to know I am deeply committed to one simple principle: this ranch is not *my* ranch, it's not *your* ranch. Gentlemen, the Bar None is *our* ranch.

About that time, Shorty Logsdon piped up, "Great! Let's sell it!"

A common problem with the English language is that sometimes you're *saying* one thing and the other person is *hearing* something else! Lena Ginster, young ranch wife over near Eagle Creek, was determined to get her two rough-and-tumble youngsters, ages six and eight, to stop cussing. It seems they'd been hanging around the corrals too much and were adopting some of the cowboy lingo. She resolved that the next time one of them swore, she'd paddle his canoe.

The next morning, the two boys came tumbling down the stairs and sat down at the breakfast table. "What'll you have," Lena asked the first one, "for breakfast?"

"Ma, I think I'll have some of them damn corn flakes!"

Well, she grabbed him, turned him over her knee and gave him a good paddling. Then she turned to the next one and demanded, "Now, what'll *you* have for breakfast?"

"I don't know ma, but I don't want none of them damn corn flakes, that's for *sure!*"

Elmer Bumpas and Boone Slick, two old retired cowmen, were sitting in a honky tonk in Willcox one night watching the young people dance and discussing the youth of today. "I swear t'God!" Elmer declared, "everything on that gal is movin' 'cept her bowels. If my ol' hoss acted that way, I'd give him worm medicine."

Boone, a man of few words, nodded in agreement.

"These young people today," Elmer continued, "they've got no morals at all."

"Yup," Boone opined.

"They hop into bed with anyone." Elmer went on, "Shucks, I didn't sleep with my wife until we was married. What about you?"

Boone massaged his whiskers, pondered for a moment, then drawled, "Can't remember, Elmer. What was her maiden name?"

Fanny Butts went to the door to answer a hard, nervous knocking. At the door stood a women in obvious despair. "Excuse me," she asked in a quivering, tearful voice, "do you own a yellow cat with a red collar?"

"Yep, I sure do. That sounds like Clancy."

"Oh dear, I'm so terribly sorry. I just ran over Clancy. Will you allow me to replace him?"

"Wel-l-l maybe," Fanny replied, her eyes narrowing, "but first tell me, how are you at catchin' mice?"

Little Humbert Rees was late for school one morning. He told his teacher he was late because he had to take the cow to the bull to be serviced.

"Couldn't you get your pa to do it?" she asked.

"No," he replied matter-of-factly, "it had to be the bull!"

On the first day of April, the Winslow drive-in theater had its annual spring opening. Just about the time the patrons were settling back to watch the main feature, the projector was turned off and a voice came through the speakers saying, "This is the manager. I'm sorry to interrupt the movie, but a man carrying a gun just left the box office. He claims his wife is here in a car with another man and he is going from car to car until he finds her. So, I'm keeping the screen dark and the lights off for one minute. And I'm asking the woman, if she's here, to leave immediately. Please! I don't want any trouble!"

It was all an April Fool's joke. The manager had arranged for two cars to speed away in the dark, to give his patrons a good laugh. But, to his amazement, seventeen cars sped off, creating the greatest traffic jam in the town's history.

Junior Frisbee was twelve years old back in the 1920s when he and his father, Newt, made a trip into Phoenix. It was the first time the two had traveled without the rest of the family and Junior was feeling real grown up. Junior loved movies and planned to go to one of the theaters along Washington Street while Newt took care of some business. "One thing, son, you must never do," his father warned. "Don't go to burlesque houses."

Naturally, Junior asked why.

"Because, you'll see things you shouldn't," his father replied.

Naturally, Junior Frisbee lost interest in seeing a movie and headed straight for a burlesque house. The cashier told him he was too young to get in, but that only made him more determined. He waited out back next to the exit door and, when a patron left, he sneaked in and sat down.

Sure enough, Junior saw something he shouldn't have seen—his father.

One summer not long ago, Prudence Neverbenhadd, maiden lady and town gossip, complained to Camp Verde constable, Wilbur Reed, that some of the town's teenagers were skinny-dipping in the Verde River, in plain view of her front porch. Nellie was a lady who wouldn't even stay in the same room with a clock that was fast. So, Wilbur went out the next day and told the youngsters to move further up stream. A few days later, the lady spoke to Wilbur again. "Haven't the kids moved?" he asked.

"They have," she snapped, "but if I go upstairs I can still see them from the window."

So the constable asked the kids to go still further away.

A week later, Miss Neverbenhadd was back in the constable's office. "They've gone upstream," she said, "but I can still see them from the attic window with spyglasses!"

Granny Bowles was learning to drive her son Willie's brand new Model T on the streets of Tucson. She ignored a stop sign and broadsided another tin lizzie. Before the echo of the crash had died away, she was out of the car with fire in her eyes. "Why don't you watch where you're goin'?" she demanded. "You're the fourth car I've hit this morning!"

As Granny Bowles approached the century mark, her friends made plans for a gala celebration. "Granny, how would you like to go for a ride in an airplane?" offered one of her great-grandchildren. "I could arrange the flight."

The old lady, who'd traveled to Arizona from Texas in a covered wagon, looked at him and said warily, "I ain't a-goin' to ride in no flying machine. I'll just sit here and watch television, like the Lord intended I should!"

The Dobbses and Roebucks had been neighbors and good friends for years. Then Elrod Dobbs and Leona Roebuck lost their spouses about the same time. After a lengthy mourning period, the two lonely ranchers decided maybe it would be better if they threw their outfits in together. But first, they decided to find out if they could agree on a few things ahead of time—one of those prenuptial meetings.

"What shall we do about the cattle?" Elrod asked.

"Let's put your brand on the cows," she said amicably, then asked, "which house shall we use?"

"Let's use your house," he replied. "It's a lot nicer than mine and we can let the foreman move his family into my old house."

"That sounds agreeable," she said pleasantly, adding, "would you like separate bedrooms or shall we share the bedroom?"

Elrod's interest cranked up several notches. "I'd prefer we use the same bedroom." He paused nervously for a moment, then added, "Would you rather we share a double bed or would you prefer twins?"

"Oh, I'd be perfectly happy to share a double bed with you," she answered.

Now came the critical question, one that Elrod had sweated over for many an evening, trying to find just the right words. "Sex!" he blurted. "How often would you like to have sex?"

"Infrequently," she calmly stated.

Elrod's eyes narrowed, and he pondered her response for a long moment, then asked cautiously, "Was that one word or two?"

Back in the days before the Mormon Temple was built in Mesa, young couples in Arizona wanting to have their marriage vows sanctified in the temple, had to take a long wagon ride to St. George, Utah. The trail was several hundred miles long, took weeks to complete and covered some of the roughest country in the whole West.

Couples started out in the rugged mountains of eastern Arizona, crossed the precipitous Mogollon Rim, then crossed the dry, windy Colorado Plateau to Lee's Ferry on the Colorado River. From there, the couple headed west to the lofty Kaibab Plateau, dropping down on the other side and further on to Pipe Springs. When they finally reached St. George and were married in the temple, the couple rested the livestock a few days, loaded up on supplies, and headed back to Arizona. It was truly a great adventure and could be dangerous if some band of Indians was on the prowl. No doubt the trip could be stressful on the nerves of these young folks.

Later in life, many of these couples regarded that hazardous journey one of the highlights of their lives. I've always believed that if those youngsters weren't well-acquainted before they left, they sure must have been by the time they returned. It could be a real test of nerves and character.

A few years ago, I interviewed an old couple, Bessie and Hiram Turley, about their experiences on the trail that became known in history as the Honeymoon Trail. "Did you ever think of divorce?" I asked Bessie.

She paused for a thoughtful moment, then replied straight-faced, "Divorce! Never. But I did consider murder on several occasions!"

Cowpunchers like to brag about their dogs almost as much as their horses. By now everyone's probably heard about Hondo Lucero's famous dog, Rumple. Ol' Rumple used to sit in the bunkhouse with the boys and play poker, however, they considered him a lousy player because he wagged his tail every time he got a winnin' hand.

Hondo used to take Rumple quail hunting, claiming that dog could go off in the brush, come back and tell you how many quail were in there.

One day a bunch of the boys went out to see for themselves. Rumple returned from the brush and scratched the ground with his paw six times. Sure enough, they went in and found six quail. A little while later, Rumple returned and scratched the ground nine times. Sure enough, when the boys went in, there were nine quail.

When they came to another brush thicket, Rumple went in for a look-see. A few minutes later, he came tearing out, all excited, with a stick in his mouth.

"What's that supposed to mean?" one of the boys asked.

Hondo merely smiled and replied, "Rumple's telling us there's more quail in there than you can shake a stick at!"

"Ol' Rumple is so smart," Hondo used to say, "when I take out my .30-.30, he tracks deer. When I pull out the shotgun, he points out the quail, and when I grab the .22, he knows he should go find some rabbits. One day I decided to fool him. I walk out the door with my fishing pole."

"What'd he do," the listener asked.

"Well, he lit out for the barn like a cut cat. I found him there, hard at work diggin' for worms."

Another time, Hondo took Rumple into the Museum Club in Flagstaff and told the bartender that his hound was so smart he could even talk. The bartender, a Californian, was typically skeptical.

"I'll bet you a drink he can talk," Hondo challenged.

"Tell him to say something," he said.

"OK, Rumple, what kind of bar is the Museum Club?"

Rumple wagged his tail and said, "Ruff, ruff!"

"See there, he says this place is 'rough, rough.' "

"Wait a minute," the bartender argued, "he didn't say anything. Let me ask a question."

Hondo shrugged and said, "Go ahead, ask him anything you like."

"Who was the greatest baseball player of all time?"

Rumple wagged his tail again and said, "Ruff, ruff!"

"He's right," Hondo laughed, "the greatest was Babe Ruth!"

"That's the biggest con game I've ever seen," the bartender shouted. "Take that dog and get out of here before I call the law."

When they got outside, Rumple looked up at Hondo with a puzzled expression and asked, "Do you think I shoulda said Mickey Mantle?"

This is not exactly a dog story, but it comes close. One year, a group of Californians came over to Cletus Robbins' ranch and asked if they could hunt quail on his land. He said that was OK, but when one started to let his hunting dogs loose, Cletus said to leave the dogs in the truck and hunt with Uncle Elam instead.

Cletus whistled and here came old Uncle Elam, skinny as a rope with long, white whiskers that hung to his chest. Boy, could he smell out those quail, slick as bear grease. He pointed 'em and fetched 'em faster and better than any dog these hunters had ever seen. They all got their limit and went home happy as a puppy with five tails.

Next year, the hunters came again, and brought along several more carloads of Californians, all anxious to see Uncle Elam hunt quail. When they got out of their car, Cletus asked, "Where's yer dogs?"

"We didn't bring 'em," one said, "we don't need dogs with old Uncle Elam!"

"Well, I'm afraid yer outta luck," Cletus said grimly, "Uncle Elam ain't with us no more."

They all started asking why and, for a while, Cletus tried to avoid the subject. Finally he gave in. "Well, if you must know," Cletus explained, "that old fool started chasing cars and got run over the other day by a truck!"

Jug Fuhr, a cowhand from Tonto Basin, was ridin' his favorite horse, Rony, in the Mazatzals when the trail gave out and both went tumbling down a steep grade. When they got to the bottom, Jug discovered one of his legs was broken and the other was pinned under a rock. "Rony, go fetch the doctor," Jug ordered. Well, ol' Rony took off on a lope for Payson, summoned a doctor, and led him to Jug. After the leg was set and bandaged, Rony carried Jug back to the ranch and put him to bed.

A few weeks later, a neighbor was remarking about what a smart horse Rony was. "He ain't so doggone smart," Jug protested, "I told him to go fetch a doctor and he brought back a veterinarian!"

Pete Arredondo had a small cow outfit down near Amado. He had this outlaw horse named Fooler. Now, ol' Fooler exhibited some of the worst traits generally attributed to humans. He was greedy, envious, devious, spiteful, superstitious, malicious, obnoxious, and stupid. Had Fooler been able to talk, he would have lied. Had he been a human, he would have committed murder just for fun.

One day Fooler pitched Pete off into a rocky arroyo strewn with cactus. Pete broke three ribs and one of his legs. Next day, he put the ornery cuss up for sale.

A young cowhand showed up at Pete's place a few days later and said, "I'd like to buy that horse you've got for sale. How much do you want for him?"

"I'll tell you how much I want for him," Pete replied, "when you tell me where you live."

"What difference does that make?" the cowboy asked. "It makes a lot of difference," Pete said. "So, where do you live?"

"Ok, I live a few miles south of Sonoita." "That's not far enough," Pete growled.

"What d'yuh mean that's not far enough?" he protested.

"Because, I'm not going to sell that damn horse to anybody who lives within 200 miles of here," Pete roared. "Not only do I never want to see this horse again, I don't even want to hear any conversations about him!"

Cecil Springer, of Seligman, was driving his old Model A Ford down Big Chino Wash towards Prescott when it suddenly quit on him. He got out, lifted the hood, and looked inside. He'd tinkered with the motor for several minutes, but couldn't figure out what was wrong. He sat down on the running board and was trying to figure out what to do next when he was startled by a deep voice behind him saying, "The coil came loose from your distributor."

Cecil looked around and saw no one, except an old yellow horse, gazing at him from behind a fence. "Who said that?" he asked suspiciously.

"I did!" the horse answered, and then repeated, "I told you, the coil came loose from your distributor. Plug it back in and she'll run good as new!"

Cecil couldn't believe what he had just witnessed. In a panic, he lit out in a run to the nearest ranch house and explained the bizarre happening to the rancher.

"Was it an old, scruffy yellar horse with a piece of his ear missin'?" the rancher asked.

"Yeah," Cecil replied excitedly, "that's the one!"

"Well, don't pay no attention to him," the rancher said calmly. "That's ol' Petey an' he don't know nothin' about cars!"

Cow people are generally so busy argurin' about the hot and dry weather in Arizona they tend to overlook the fact that it gets pretty cold in the northern part of the state. Folks don't leave their brass monkeys out overnight in the wintertime, that's for dang sure! One year it got so cold up there on the Double A outfit, north of Williams, that Harvey Culpepper found a whole nest of rattlesnakes frozen out straight as ramrods. He pounded 'em into the ground and used 'em as fence posts. Harvey thought he was real resourceful until spring came. The snakes thawed and crawled off with sixteen miles of barbed wire!

Ethan Merkle, a rancher out near Mormon Lake, took his nephew, Twist, out duck hunting on the lake one afternoon. He was most anxious to show the kid what a great shot he was. They'd sat out there in the cold, damp weather for about an hour, when finally a solitary duck flew overhead. Ethan raised his shotgun, took careful aim, and fired. But the duck kept right on going until he was out of sight. Finally, Ethan turned to his nephew and said matter-of-factly, "Twist, you've just witnessed a miracle. There goes a dead duck!"

Tomas Corral was out mending one of his fences when a huge Cadillac with longhorns mounted on the hood pulled up in a cloud of dust. A big man wearing a tall stetson, high-heel boots, and with a sagging belly, stepped out and said, "Howdy, pard. Is this y'all's ranch?"

"Sure is," Tomas smiled agreeably.

"How bigga spread y'all got here?" the big fella asked.

"Well, it starts over at that corner, and runs down to that big cottonwood tree. And, from there, it runs down that fence line to that corner over yonder, then back to that clump of brush and back here."

"That's a pretty small piece of ground," the big fella opined. "Do you wanna know how big my spread is?"

"Do I have a choice?" Tomas said to himself.

"I can get in my car," the big fella said boastfully, "and start out first thing in the morning, drive all day and not get to the first corner. What do you think about that?"

"Yeah," Tomas said matter-of-factly, "I used to have a car like that myself!"

A newspaperman was interviewing John Ed Puckle after he won the multimillion dollars on the roulette wheel at Las Vegas, correctly picking the number 12. "How'd you come up with the lucky number?" the scribe asked. "Did you have to do some fancy calculating?"

"No," John Ed replied matter-of-factly, "I had a dream where I saw this big number 9. Then the next night, it was turned upside down to a 6. So, I used my brains and added up 9 and 6 and got 12, and that's how I won!"

Zeke Bunch, local insurance salesman in Holbrook, was trying to sell some insurance to Poke Raney, a local cowboy. Poke was being stubborn so Zeke decided to apply the hard sell. "Poke, don't you want your wife to be able to carry on after your gone?"

Poke pondered that for a moment then declared indignantly, "I don't feel obligated to finance any carrying
on she might do after I'm gone!"

My old friend Maggie Wilson tells about a fella from
Globe named Andre Maurel, who was mighty proud of
his peach orchard. He sold the peaches at the market and
was understandably miffed when pranksters pilfered
them off the trees. The pranksters, in this case, were the
miners who passed his orchard on their way to work.

The street next to his place ran from town up to the
mine. The bindle stiffs would blatantly help themselves.
Andre's prime peaches seemed to go well with whatever

else mama had loaded up in the lunch pail that morning. He warned the miners to leave his orchard alone, but they just laughed, so he decided to take matters into his own hands.

He went down to the drug store and bought some croton oil, a strong purgative, along with a needle and a syringe. The resourceful Frenchman then methodically injected every peach on the tree nearest the road, the miner's favorite one to pluck. Andre smiled mirthfully the next day as the miners once again helped themselves to his peaches.

It is a historical fact that every one of those miners spent all night and the next day, and the next, camped out in some outdoor privy. The company had to shut down operations for three days. Not even the miner's union had been able to accomplish that!

Andre Maurel goes down in history as the only man to singlehandedly shut down a mine and live to tell about it!

Speaking of Globe, the citizens of that mining community completed their new Central School before realizing it was located near a popular bawdy house. The law in Globe required that a parlor house couldn't exist within 400 feet of a school, so the good citizens petitioned the sheriff to close the house. Another group of concerned citizens rose to the occasion to defend the house, claiming it was there first.

The obliging sheriff borrowed a cowboy's rope and measured the distance between the two structures and found the 400 foot limit extended three feet into the parlor of the bawdy house. The sheriff settled the issue with the wisdom of a frontier Solomon when he declared the madam had to confine all activities to the back rooms—which were within the legal limit.

Wimpy Halstead was foreman for the Lazy J outfit and had a reputation for being hard to work for. One day he was interviewin' a new cowhand named Billy Buck. "Billy," he said, "I'm a man of few words. If I say come, you come—savvy?"

Billy looked him square in the eye and replied, "Wimpy, I'm a man of few words, too! If I shake my head, I ain't comin'!"

President George Bush was jogging along the beach near his Kinnebunkport vacation home recently when he stumbled across a bottle, half-buried in the sand. He reached down, picked it up, and a magic genie suddenly popped out. "I recognize you!" the genie said. "You're the President of the United States. I'm going to grant you any wish you choose!"

The President thought about that for a moment, then hauled out a map of the Middle East. "See this?" he said, unfolding the map. "Here is Iraq, this is Israel, over here is Syria, there is Iran. Genie, this area has been a thorn in my side for some time. My wish is that you would bring peace to the entire region."

The genie stroked his chin and responded, "I'm sorry, but that's an impossible request. That one can't be done. You'll have to choose something else."

The President thought for another long moment then said. "Well, there is something else. Down in the Southwest is a place called Arizona. For the past few years, there's been a lot of political turmoil. My wish is that you would restore some harmony to the place!"

The genie pondered that one, stroked his chin once again, and said, "Let me see that map of the Middle East again!"

PART TWO

Wild & Woolly

CHAPTER 15

The Baldheaded Fox
of Ol' Willcox

Robbing trains in southern Arizona became quite fashionable among border outlaws around the turn of the century. A few qualified as comic opera.

Joe George and Grant Wheeler, a couple of unemployed cowboys, held up the Southern Pacific and tried to blow up the safe in the express car with dynamite. They packed too big a charge around it and blew the train car to splinters. Worse, they'd found several sacks of silver coin in the car and used them for ballast. When the dynamite exploded, silver pesos went flying all over southern Arizona. To make matters worse for the would-be desperados, when the smoke cleared, they discovered the safe was empty. The only loot on the train had been blown away.

Another time, Doc Smart and his gang robbed a train near Pantano, then made their getaway on the steam engine. They rode it to the outskirts of Tucson, then put it in reverse and jumped off. A posse found the pilfered locomotive a few miles from town and couldn't figure out how the culprits got away without leaving any tracks. Detectives weren't able to solve the mystery of the vanishing train robbers until some time later when one of the gang members was captured. He explained that the engine had gone backwards down the track from Tucson until it'd run out of steam.

Burt Alvord is best remembered in the history of outlawry as a gregarious constable who moonlighted as a train robber. Before his luck ran out, Burt had masterminded two spectacular train robberies, one at Cochise and the other at Fairbank.

Burt was a pretty good lawman and absolutely fearless, but figured he'd never earn enough money keeping the peace to buy that cattle ranch he'd always wanted. He was also convinced that nobody would ever suspect the town marshal of robbing a train, especially him.

You see, Burt had an IQ that roughly matched his age and was therefore certain that nobody would believe him smart enough to plan and execute a daring train robbery. Most folks thought the closest Burt ever came to a brainstorm was a light drizzle. He'd have to be out of *his* mind to get an idea, they said. But, when the Southern Pacific was robbed at Cochise, railroad detectives suspected Burt as the ringleader. Most folks around Willcox disagreed, however, saying that Burt was not bright enough to be involved in such a dastardly deed. Burt obligingly agreed with locals.

Burt not only led the gang who robbed the train at Cochise, he also organized and led a posse in pursuit of himself, something quite unique in the annals of outlawry.

Burt was feeling so confident that, a few weeks later, he organized another robbery, this one at the railroad station in Fairbank. He might have continued these escapades had it not been for one of his henchmen, Three-Finger Jack Dunlap, who fingered him after the gang bungled the train robbery at Fairbank. Burt's brief career as a master planner of train robbery had come to an abrupt end.

Burt Alvord was a short, baldheaded fellow, with an easy grin, swarthy complexion, and a big mustache. He seldom bathed. He was also a shiftless rowdy who spent most of his time hanging out with barflies of similar persuasion, hustling quarters in the pool halls around town. A good-natured buffoon, his main interests were guns, horses, and pool halls. Burt also loved practical jokes. When he wasn't keeping the peace, or breaking it, he was dreaming up some practical joke.

Once, he and a pal, Matt Burts, sent a telegram to friends in Tombstone announcing that the "Bodies of Burt Alvord and Matt Burts will arrive on the afternoon stage." This bit of startling news had all the locals in a state of remorse, for the two boys had grown up in the town and were quite popular among the rounders along Allen Street. Burt had a rather coarse sense of humor, to match the rest of his rough-hewn character and, if locals had stopped to think about it, they should have suspected a practical joke all along.

All day the locals were sitting around thinking up good things to say about the lads, something quite difficult, since neither had any redeeming qualities. Still, when people die, regardless of how useless they were, folks feel obliged to say something nice about them.

A large number of townsfolk turned out to meet the stage expecting to see a couple of wooden boxes strapped to the top. They were somewhat dumbfounded to see Burt and Matt climb down out of the stage wearing broad grins. "Sure, our bodies arrived," they laughed. "We never go anywhere without them."

The townsfolk found little humor in the incident. Even the *Tombstone Epitaph* scolded the boys in print the next day. But that little prank paled by comparison to the next one Burt had up his sleeve. He and Biddy Doyle, a diminutive ex-wrestler and pugilist, who would do anything for money except work, went down to Bisbee to stir up a little mischief. They spread word along Brewery Gulch that Biddy was looking for a wrestling match. A big, but not-too-bright Cornish "Cousin Jack" was selected to be Biddy's opponent. Burt and Biddy then began taking bets. Next, they had to find a suitable place to hold the match. The softest ground in Bisbee turned out to be the huge manure pile in front of the Copper Queen Mine. This was before the days of mechanical cars and mules were used to pull the ore cars.

With interest thus inspired, the sporting crowds of both Bisbee and Tombstone showed up in great numbers. The place was so crowded you couldn't cuss a cat without gettin' hair in your mouth. By the time the match was ready to begin, the odds were ten to one in favor of the big Cornishman. Burt, who was acting as trainer, then persuaded the big man to take a fall. He agreed, for a small fee, then the two conspirators bet all their money on Biddy.

The choreography for the match was poorly planned. They should have made it look good for a few rounds. The pair had wrestled around in the manure only a few brief moments when Biddy did a very unsportsmanlike thing. He suddenly rammed the Cornishman's head down, face first, into the mule dung, causing the big guy to give up immediately. The fix might have worked had the big miner not thrown in the towel so fast. While the crowd was in a state of stunned confusion, Burt and Biddy took their winnings and slipped quickly through the crowd to the edge of town where they'd picketed a couple of fast horses. Thus mounted, they hightailed it out of town with a mob of angry bettors hot on their heels.

Such mischievous antics were bound to lead to a serious life of crime. And they did. As mentioned earlier, Burt decided to supplement his income by robbing the Southern Pacific. He got caught and did some time in the territorial prison at Yuma.

After that first robbery at Cochise, Burt took charge of the loot and hid it somewhere around Willcox. It was never found. Upon his release from prison, Burt headed back to Willcox. He hung around town for a few days visiting with some of his old cronies and then vanished.

Down along the Mexican border, old-timers swore that Burt went to South America, bought a big cattle ranch, got married, and settled down.

Maybe Burt was a lot smarter than folks gave him credit.

CHAPTER 16

The Glorious Bareback Ride of Climax Jim

Lady Godiva's famous ride through Coventry might be an English classic, but she had nothing on (no pun intended here) a notorious Arizona rustler named Climax Jim. That famous lady rode nude through only one town. Climax Jim rode through two in his birthday suit.

It all happened back in 1899, when Jim was locked up in the Springerville jail for stealing a herd of cows. Just before his trial, Jim asked for and received a fresh change of clothes. While in a state of undress, he looked out the window and spotted a horse tied to a hitching post. Now this was an opportunity too good to let pass by. Jim figured that if he took the time to dress, the horse might be gone. So, he ran out of the house stark naked and leaped upon the horse, kicked the startled animal in the ribs, and hightailed it out of Springerville, heading for Eager, about a mile further south. Beyond Eager lay the rugged White Mountains and freedom.

Old-timers around Eager claimed Climax Jim streaked through town that day wearing nothing but a determined look. A posse from Springerville took up the chase but Jim escaped—barely.

Climax Jim's outrageous behavior was a favorite topic of newspaper writers around the turn of the century, who followed his misadventures with great curiosity. He had a knack for getting himself in and out of mischief. Now, a lot of people have been able to talk their way out of trouble, but Jim was able to literally chew his way out of a pinch.

Climax Jim never met a cow he didn't like. He was an unabashed cow thief. In his mind, he was an entrepreneur. He'd ride upon a herd of range cattle and convince himself that he was merely gathering them for the owner. If nobody came around, he'd take it upon himself to drive the herd a ways, all the time thinking he was doin' the rancher a favor by keepin' the cows gathered. After he'd ridden some distance and the owner still hadn't showed, he'd stop, build a little fire, fan it real hard with his hat, then heat up a runnin' iron and add his own rendering of cow pyrography. He justified all this by claimin' this was how other great cattle barons got their start.

One time, he stole a herd of cattle over in Apache County, altered their brands, and drove them to Clifton where he sold them to a local butcher. Then he came upon a novel idea. Why not double his profit by altering the check as well. Well, the law caught up with Climax Jim, not for stealing cows, but for altering the brand on the butcher's check.

He was known far and wide as a cattle thief extraordinaire so no one should have been too surprised when the county prosecuting attorney denounced him as the most dangerous criminal in the whole territory. The defense attorney was, of course, outraged at the flagrant use of such strong language against his client, so he jumped up and indignantly engaged the prosecutor in a shouting match.

During the confusion, when all attention was focused on the two attorneys, Climax Jim spotted Exhibit A, the altered check and the only evidence against him, setting on a table in front of the bench. He reached over, picked it up, and stuffed it in his mouth, which was chock-full of chewing tobacco.

When order was returned to the courtroom, the judge asked for Exhibit A. Climax Jim sat pensively chewing his tobacco while the prosecuting attorney and his staff searched in vain for the missing check. Finally, the defendant was called to stand before the judge while he dismissed the charges for lack of evidence.

Climax Jim smiled innocently, sayin' "Thank ya judge." Then, with all the aplomb of a muleskinner, spit a curious-looking wad into the cuspidor and strolled casually out of the courtroom, a free man once again.

CHAPTER 17

Chinese Gunfighters

Pinal City was a boisterous boom town located near Superior at the site of the present-day Boyce Thompson Southwest Arboretum. Born in boom, died in adobe dust, there's little left of the long-deserted remains. But during its heyday, the place was a smelter town for one of Arizona's richest mines, the fabulous Silver King. And, for a brief spell, it was one of the wildest.

The participants in Pinal City's most memorable gunfight are among the most unusual in the annals of Arizona history. That's because the participants didn't have familiar-sounding names of gunslinger lore like Johnny Ringo, Doc Holliday, or Buckskin Frank Leslie. This particular shootout was an all-Chinese affair and the participants names were Qui Gee, Go Chu, Dang Fook, and Wang Wy.

The fight started over a poker game. Qui Gee thought he was being cheated so he jerked out his six-shooter and plugged Go Chu. Then Go Chu's pals, Dang Fook and

Wang Wy, pulled out their six-guns and gave Qui Gee a bad case of lead poisoning. They were last seen headed out of town on a dead run with a posse in hot pursuit. It isn't known for certain whether or not their getaway was successful.

Go Chu's friends wanted him to have an American-style funeral. Since the town had neither a Bible nor a preacher, they hired a local bartender to perform the service. He donned a dark broadcloth coat and, in a prayerful tone, read a passage from Shakespeare's *Romeo and Juliet.*

Go Chu's friends were so impressed they chipped in forty dollars in gold coin. Afterwards the funeral party retreated to the nearest saloon and the bartender set up drinks for everybody.

CHAPTER 18

"It's Déjà Vu All Over Again"

During the latter part of the 19th century, energetic Arizonans promoting statehood worked tirelessly to assure the rest of the country that the territory was no longer a lawless frontier overrun with desperados and highwaymen. Easterners took great delight in bashing Arizona, claiming early on that too many Mexicans lived here. That struck the locals as kinda odd since this land had been a part of Mexico before the United States took it over. Then they claimed the place had too many Mormons. But what caused raised eyebrows in the East the most was the perception that the place was crawling with lawless bandits.

It seems that every time statehood promoters convinced our Eastern cousins that Arizona was about ready for statehood, some galoot would go and spoil things. Like the time back in 1888 when Jim Brazelton held up the Tucson-Florence stage. He didn't get away with much cash and it might have been quickly forgotten had there not been a newspaperman on board. John Clum, former editor of the *Tombstone Epitaph* , was an eyewitness and wrote a colorful account of the event. Naturally, the story made the newspapers back East and attracted a lot of attention locally.

The following week the stage made the same run. This time it was filled with curious tourists who wanted to see where the famous robbery occurred. It was a revelous group of thrill-seekers on the stage that day and, when they neared the site where the stage was robbed, the passengers grew anxious. "Show us where the desperado appeared," one asked.

The driver pulled up the horses and pointed out towards a large bush. "It was right over there. He hid behind that bush," the driver declared. And, with a look of startled surprise, added, "And, by God, there he is again."

It was déjà vu all over again. This time Brazelton's victims were wealthy tourists and the haul was considerable. The media loved it and Arizona's lawless reputation remained intact.

CHAPTER 19

Jailhouse Rock

In the rough and tumble towns of early Arizona, churches and jails were most conspicuous by their absence. Holbrook became the county seat of Navajo County in 1895 and didn't get around to erecting a church until 1914. During that time, it claimed to be the only county seat in the United States that didn't have one.

At the other end of the frontier social spectrum were jails. Most of these early day *calabozos* were made of adobe and the inmates could dig their way out with very little effort. Since the majority of scoundrels were locked up for public drunkenness, and were turned loose after they sobered up, it didn't seem to make much difference anyway.

Overcrowding was a problem, even in those days. One saturday night in Jerome, the jail was filled with drunks so the remaining were chained to a large mill wheel.

The next morning, the thirsty imbibers picked up the wheel and carried it down to the nearest saloon and demanded an ax to widen the door so they could haul it inside.

The citizens of Wickenburg chained their rowdies to a big mesquite tree. When the tree became overcrowded, usually every saturday night, the surplus were chained to a huge log.

One night, Big George Sayers, a notorious reprobate from Gunsight, became drunk and disorderly. After a long struggle, he was finally chained up to the log. Big George had the dubious reputation of possessing the most lurid, creative, and varied vocabulary in the entire territory. It was said he would lie awake at night inventing new oaths which he would languish on dogs, people, his horse, all animate and inanimate objects he might encounter.

He awoke the next morning unrepented, thirsty, and bellowing like a range bull, awakening the whole town and half the county. When nobody responded, Big George took matters into his own hands, shouldering the log and heading for the nearest saloon. He demanded a drink and, incidentally, he got it.

George's voice could sidetrack a cyclone. Another time, when he was jumped by a mountain lion, George turned and let out a howl that petrified that lion in his tracks. Then, he took it into Gunsight and put it in the park as a statue. He used to fish by standing on the bank and letting out a loud bellow. The shock stunned the fish and they'd rise to the surface where George could wade out and pick out the big ones. He always got his limit.

When the citizens of Clifton finally got around to building a jail they wanted it to be escapeproof. So they hired a hard-rock miner named Margarito Varela to carve one out of solid rock. When he was finished, Varela took his pay and headed for the nearest saloon where he proposed a toast to the "World's Greatest Jail Builder." Apparently the other imbibers weren't impressed and refused to toast, whereupon Varela got angry, pulled his six-shooter and shot a hole in the ceiling. They pounced upon him and carted him off to the *calabozo*. The "World's Greatest Jail Builder" became the first inmate in the jail he built.

GRAHAM

Justice was much more practical and expedient on the Arizona frontier than it is today. Take, for instance, Tucson. During the 1860s, the Old Pueblo was being terrorized by a bunch of scoundrels who'd been chased out of California by vigilantes. Captain John C. Cremony wrote in his classic book, *Life Among the Apaches*, that southern Arizona was "cursed by the presence of two or three hundred of the most infamous scoundrels it is possible to conceive. Innocent and unoffending men were shot down or bowie-knifed merely for the pleasure of witnessing their death agonies. Men walked the streets and public squares with double-barreled shotguns, and hunted each other as sportsmen hunt for game."

Tucson wasn't exactly the kind of community where one would want to raise a family. So city fathers, led by businessman Mark Aldrich, decided upon a novel idea to rid the town of these unwanted troublemakers for good.

Since Tucson had no suitable jail, a public whipping post was set up in the plaza. The standard punishment for crimes was a public whipping. But there was a catch. The culprits would be given their punishment in two doses on successive Saturdays. Following a speedy trial, the town marshal would give the rascals a severe public spanking. Afterwards, they were told to come back next Saturday for the second installment.

It goes without saying that when the following Saturday rolled around, those villains made sure they were a long ways from Tucson.

CHAPTER 20

The Day Wyatt Got Caught with His Pants Down

Hollywood's traditional rendering of the Western gun-fight was a dramatic confrontation between frontier stalwarts. The one wearing the white hat was the good guy and the mustachioed, mean-eyed one in the black hat was bad. They squared off on main street at high noon with each encouraging the other to draw first. The bad guy always drew first but the good guy always won. Some-times he got a flesh wound in the shoulder, but it healed in a day or two.

The closest thing to one of those movie renditions was the so-called "Gunfight at OK Corral" when the Earp brothers and their pal, Doc Holliday, faced off against Tom and Frank McLaury and their cohort, young Billy Clanton. Even then the real event was largely forgotten at first, probably because it lacked a catchy title.

The celebrated fight on October 26, 1881 didn't occur at the OK Corral. It was over on Fremont Street between the Harwood house and Fly's photo gallery. Aficionados are eternally grateful to the pulp writer who arbitrarily changed the location of the fight to the corral. Somehow, "Gunfight Over on Fremont Street Between the Harwood House and Fly's Photo Gallery," doesn't inspire.

Gunfights in the real West, as opposed to reel West, were usually lacking in flamboyance and gallantry. Poor marksmanship was common in frontier showdowns.

Thirty-four shots were exchanged at the OK Corral, with each side getting off an equal number. Clay Allison once remarked sagely, "speed is fine, but accuracy is final." When the smoke cleared, the Clanton-McLaury bunch had scored only three hits in seventeen tries, while shots fired by the Earps and Doc Holliday found their mark eleven times.

In another frontier fracas, Kansas saloonkeeper Rowdy Joe Lowe, while defending his wife Rowdy Kate's virtue, swapped fifty shots with an antagonist named Sweet, before scoring a hit. In 1879, in Dodge City's famous Long Branch Saloon, a buffalo hunter named Levi Richardson fired five bullets at a gambler named Cockeyed Frank Loving. Levi was close enough to Cock-eyed Frank to have picked his pocket, but missed all five tries. Loving wasn't much better. He fired three times, finally hitting Levi with a fatal shot from a distance of just two feet.

Cock-eyed Frank's aim didn't improve with age. Three years later, he was engaged in another shootout where sixteen shots were exchanged with neither side scoring a hit. They called a halt to the festivities, perhaps because of darkness, and resumed action the following day. In the replay between the two, Cockeye's poor shooting finally caught up with him and he bit the dust.

Reputations were often built on heresy and tall tales. By the time Bat Masterson left the Old West and headed for New York City to become a sports writer, he was being credited with killing thirty-one men. In reality, he'd killed only one and that was after the man had shot him first. Later, Bat habitually purchased new Colt revolvers, carved notches on the handles, and presented them to friends, telling each it was the six-gun he carried when he was a famous lawman.

The legend of Wild Bill Hickock, the self-styled "Prince of Pistoleers," began soon after he ambushed and killed three unarmed Nebraska farmers. He managed to escape the hangman's noose and, as the story was told and retold by Wild Bill, the three unarmed Nebraska farmers were miraculously transformed into ten members of the notorious McCanles Gang. Wild Bill slew all ten in the cause of justice.

When seen in retrospect, some frontier gunfights were downright comic opera. Back in 1906, Arizona Ranger Harry Wheeler was called upon to arrest one J.A. Tracy in Benson, after the latter had been charged with threatening his former girlfriend and her new husband. They faced off on main street, Hollywood-style, with both Tracy and Wheeler going for their six-guns. Each fired four times. Tracy missed on all four tries, Ranger Wheeler, a crack shot, scored four hits.

"I'm all done in," Tracy called out as he dropped his gun arm to his side. Wheeler laid his empty pistol down and rushed to aid the stricken man. But Tracy wasn't "done in" yet. He raised his revolver and fired twice, hitting Wheeler in the leg and foot. The resourceful Ranger picked up the only weapon available, a handful of rocks, and hurled them at Tracy.

Years later Wheeler humorously recalled the incident: "I'll never know how it happened," he said, "only four cylinders of my gun were loaded. So, when I was out of ammunition, I dropped my gun and started throwing rocks at the fellow."

It's hard to imagine a Hollywood director giving serious consideration to the Wheeler-Tracy gunfight on the silver screen.

Wyatt Earp was a victim of what might be called Murphy's Law in a shootout that has attracted little attention among mythmakers. In the unsung aftermath of the "Gunfight at OK Corral," several participants in the feud became victims of a bloody vendetta. Virgil Earp was the first to fall to an assassin's bullet. He was critically wounded in an ambush on the streets of Tombstone. A few months later, Morgan Earp was drygulched while shooting a game of pool in Hatch's saloon in the "Town Too Tough To Die."

A vengeful Wyatt Earp recruited a few trusted friends to join him on a manhunt for his brother's killers. Frank Stilwell, one of the bushwhackers, was gunned down in Tucson. Charlie Cruz, who acted as lookout when Stilwell killed Morgan, was the next victim. Then, acting on a tip, Wyatt learned the notorious Curly Bill Brocius and some of his gang were camped at Mescal Springs, a stage station on the western slopes of the Whetstone Mountains. Brocius, a boisterous, curly-headed Irishman, had become godfather of the outlaw element in Cochise County after Old Man Clanton died of an acute case of lead poisoning.

Wyatt and his friends rode out to Mescal Springs, about thirty-five miles west of Tombstone, on March 21, 1882. In order to make the long ride more comfortable, Wyatt loosened his gunbelt. They approached the springs about midday and Wyatt dismounted to check for sign. He walked over a rise and stumbled into the outlaw camp. Neither side was expecting company. Wyatt's cronies, who were riding behind, put their spurs to their mounts and rode helter-skelter for cover leaving him to face the gang alone. Curly Bill grabbed a shotgun and fired at close range, sending a double load of buckshot that tore off a piece of Wyatt's coattail. The chagrined outlaw then angrily hurled the empty gun, narrowly missing Earp. Wyatt was also packing a scattergun. His shotgun roared sending two rounds of buckshot into Curly Bill's midsection.

After the outlaw chieftain bit the dust, Wyatt turned his attention to the other desperados. During the confusion, they were ducking and dodging, firing wildly as they ran for cover. Wyatt dropped the empty shotgun and reached for his pistol but, during the excitement, he'd forgotten the loosened belt. Gunbelt and pants had fallen down around his ankles. Wyatt's horse, spooked by the gunfire, was rearing wildly. While the outlaws took potshots from a grove of cottonwoods, Wyatt tried gamely to calm his horse, pull up his pants, and locate his trusty six-shooter. The outlaws took advantage of Wyatt's precarious situation to make their getaway.

Hollywood probably wouldn't be interested in that gunfight, either.

CHAPTER 21

Famous Last Words

Old-timers used to claim a man's true character, or lack of, came out at his hanging. Some tough hombres walked boldly up the scaffold and took their medicine without a whimper. Other rascals, who'd shown their victims no mercy, bawled and pleaded as they took their final walk. A few took that final *paseo* to the next gatherin' in a bravado manner as devil-may-care as the life they'd led.

Notorious train robber, Black Jack Ketchum, during a ten-year crime spree that netted a quarter of a million dollars, was finally captured and sentenced to hang in Clayton, New Mexico on April 26, 1901. Train robbery was a hanging offense in those days. Black Jack, an unwitting creature of habit, was arrested after robbing the train near Twin Mountains, New Mexico for the fourth time. "I'm going to die as I lived," he told the padre. "Have someone play a fiddle when I swing off."

On the morning of his hanging, Black Jack danced up the scaffold, assisted the hangman in adjusting his noose, and told the audience he'd be in hell before they had breakfast.

In 1902, at Solomonville, Arizona, Augustine Chacon stood on the scaffolding and gave a thirty-minute speech that would have done a tree-stumping politician proud. Afterwards, friends and well-wishers stepped up to shake hands. He turned the last one back, saying, "It's too late now. Time to hang." As they slipped the noose around his neck, he shouted "Adios todos amigos."

Some thought the crafty old outlaw's speech was an attempt to lull his audience into a slumber before making an escape. They had good cause to be apprehensive. During an earlier escape, he'd used his pretty girlfriend to distract the jailer and a mariachi band to drown out the hacksaw blade as he noisily sawed his way to freedom.

Some never lost their sense of humor, despite the grim circumstances in which they found themselves. In Tucson, as they were draping the noose around his neck, Joe Casey mused, "Very uncomfortable necktie, boys." At his hanging, George Shears casually remarked "Gentlemen, I am not used to this business, having never been hung before. Do I jump off or slide off?"

During the Christmas season of 1883 in Bisbee, five men—Red Sample, Dan Dowd, Bill Delaney, Dan Kelly, and Tex Howard—robbed the Goldwater-Castenada store. During the heist, they shot and killed four people. They were captured shortly after, tried, and sentenced to hang on the following March 8 at the county courthouse in Tombstone. It was the largest mass hanging in Arizona history.

Just before the hanging, prizefighter John L. Sullivan visited Tombstone to put on a boxing exhibition. The condemned men asked great John L. to pay them a visit and he obliged. The "Boston Strong Boy" was somewhat at a loss for words when Dan Dowd grinned and said, "John L. Sullivan, you think you are a great man because you can knock out one man in five rounds. But our sheriff here, who is much smaller than you, is gonna to knock out five men in one round."

At 1 p.m. on the day of the hanging, all five men were led up the scaffolding and had nooses placed around their necks by Sheriff J. W. Ward. All five wore smiles on their faces, waved to friends in the crowd, and shook hands with officers and the local padre. Sheriff Ward then asked the men if they had any last words. Dowd replied, "It's getting pretty hot sheriff so you might as well get on with it." Tex Howard turned to his cohort with a macabre expression and said, "Quit complainin' Dan, it's liable to get a whole lot hotter where we're goin'."

Another member of that infamous gang that held up the Goldwater-Casteneda store was John Heith. Since he only helped *plan* the robbery, Heith demanded and got a separate trial. He was sentenced to a term at the Yuma Territorial Prison.

The outraged citizens of Bisbee and Tombstone decided to take the law into their own hands. On the morning of February 22, 1884, they took Heith from his cell and gave him a suspended sentence—from a telegraph pole on Toughnut Street.

Since lynching is a serious crime, the case had to be investigated. The county coroner was the colorful Tombstone physician, Dr. George Goodfellow. It was a good bet that many of Doc's friends were among the group of vigilantes that hung John Heith. Nearly everybody agreed that Heith got what he deserved, but Doc Goodfellow was determined to do his sworn duty as coroner. With the wisdom of a frontier Solomon, Doc declared that the deceased came to his demise as a result of shortage of breathing while at a high altitude. Case closed.

History failed to record the last remarks of a desperado who loved to twirl his pistol by the trigger guard. He innocently claimed two men he murdered in cold blood doing his twirl were *accidents*. Judge Lynch and his hung jury took charge and administered another of those suspended sentences to the culprit. Next morning, he was found hanging from the limb of a cottonwood tree with a note attached saying, *"This was no accident."*

PART THREE

As Big as All Outdoors

CHAPTER 22

The Night They Burned Ol' Prescott Down

Montezuma Street in Prescott will always be better known by its familiar nickname "Whiskey Row." The row had as many as forty saloons lining the west side of the street back in the days before prohibition. On Saturday nights, the town was noisier than three jackasses in a tin barn. Actually, Prescott's first whiskey row wasn't on Montezuma Street, but was located a block west along Granite Creek. According to local legend, the first saloon, called the Quartz Rock, was run by an army deserter who'd lost his nose in a brawl.

The reason the row was moved up to Montezuma Street is anybody's guess. Some old-timers say it's because sober citizens got tired of hauling drunks out of the creek. Others claim it was because the sight of all that pure water in Granite Creek made the boozehounds sick to their stomachs.

Granite Street, which ran beside the creek, was also the town's designated "red-light district." A few years ago, the old parlor houses along the south end of the street were torn down to make way for an athletic field at the new high school. Prescott historian Budge Ruffner, says that during construction an old-timer wandered over and asked the workers what they were building. One of the men explained they were going to build a new boy's playground. The old man thought about that for a moment then dryly declared, "That's what it's always been."

$$\psi \quad \psi \quad \psi$$

It was a warm, sultry summer night in Prescott that July 14 of the year 1900. Saturday nights in Prescott during those days were as wild as a roomful of turpentined cats. The honky-tonk saloons and gambling casinos along Whiskey Row were busier than a one-armed man trying to saddle a bronc. Everyone was welcome except pacifists. The sounds of the rinky-tink pianos could be heard throughout the town. The joints were crawling with boisterous, devil-may-care prospectors, cowboys, and saloon girls out to celebrate another Prescott saturday night. It was a perfect night to separate some poor sucker from his poke sack.

At the Palace Bar, a cowboy stepped across the body of a fellow cowpuncher sprawled on the floor. "Give me the same but make it a double," he demanded. Several drinks later, he made a wager he could fly. Bets were placed and he climbed atop the bar and leaped off, flapping his arms wildly. He landed on the floor with a loud thud that sobered him up considerably. Getting up slowly, he looked at his pals and asked, "Why'd ya let me do it?"

"We thought ya could," one replied disappointedly. "I lost ten bucks on ya."

Yavapai County's colorful sheriff, George Ruffner, remarked drily, "To jail all the drunks in Prescott tonight, you'd have to put a roof over the whole town."

❖ ❖ ❖

Down at the south end of Whiskey Row at the Scopel Hotel, a careless hard-rock miner had jammed his pick candle into the wall of his hotel room and, in his rush to join in the festivities, forgot to extinguish it. A fire started and the hotel was quickly engulfed in flames. Volunteer fire companies rushed to fight the fire which had spread to the drinking establishments on the Row.

At the Palace Bar, the customers gallantly picked up the beautiful mahogany backbar and all its liquid contents, along with the piano and carried them across the street to the plaza. Others hauled roulette wheels and faro tables to the plaza. A barber chair was carried over to the bandstand.

So while bright orange flames licked the sky over Prescott, gambling resumed, the barbershop re-opened, the relocated Palace Bar sold drinks, and the piano player belted out tunes. The most requested song was naturally, "There'll Be a Hot Time in the Old Town Tonight!"

❖

CHAPTER 23

Don't Nobody Horse Around with Joe's Mule

Back in the 1870s, Joe Felmer was a colorful scout for the army at old Camp Grant. When he wasn't out on the campaign trail riding for General George Crook, Felmer operated a small ranch on the San Pedro River. For several months, Apaches had been raiding his pastures and running off with his horses and mules. And he was itching to get even.

One day, Joe was at the post watching an auction of unserviceable mules when a bright idea struck. If the plan worked, he'd make a sitting target of the next Apache who tried to ride off on one of his mules.

When Felmer made the only bid on Lazarus, the laziest, most stubborn army mule in Arizona, his friends laughed and claimed the desert heat must have baked his brain. Felmer figured to let them have their little laugh now, for he'd surely have the last one.

He knew the useless mule wouldn't be rode. That's what he was counting on. The next Apache that raided his ranch and tried to ride off on old Lazarus was going to be a sitting target. Felmer let the old mule graze peacefully in the pasture while he waited anxiously for the next Apache raid.

Sure enough, three days later a youngster came running up to Joe's ranch house yelling excitedly that three Apaches had climbed upon Lazarus' back and were trying to make a getaway. Joe quickly grabbed his rifle and ran towards the pasture.

The scheme was working perfectly. The old mule was standing firm while three Apaches were kicking away wildly with their heels. Joe smiled and cranked a shell into his rifle. But, just as he got ready to fire, the quick-thinking Apache on the rear jerked off his sash, strung it up under the mule's tail and began sawing furiously back and forth. Suddenly, the dullness left Lazarus' eyes, his ears perked up and, as if by some miracle, he seemed to have regained the vigor of his youth. He lit out across the desert, dodging cactus and jumping arroyos.

Much to his disgust, Felmer didn't even get off a shot. The last anyone saw of Lazarus, he was leaving the country with three Apaches hanging on for dear life.

CHAPTER 24

The Dally Man

As a general rule, ropers east of the Rockies tied hard and fast. Hard and fast roping had its origins in Texas where a roper tosses a loop around a cow's horns while the other end of the rope was anchored to the saddle horn. The main drawback was that if there was more wild cow than you bargained for, you and your horse might get dragged clear to the next county.

The other style, used further west, was the dally. Dally came from the Mexican *dar la vuelta* or, "to take a turn" around the saddle horn. Dar la vuelta was corrupted twice by the gringos. First it was "dolly welter," then, simply "dally."

A dally roper held the loose end of the rope in one hand and after making the catch, took a couple of turns around the saddle horn just before the slack came out of the rope. The main drawback to dally roping was that if one of the roper's fingers or thumb got caught between the rope and the saddle horn as the slack came out of the rope, it was *adios* finger or thumb. It was the slickest amputation you ever saw. That's why so many old dally ropers are missing parts of their fingers.

In her wonderful book, *Hashknife Cowboy*, Stella Hughes tells a story worth retelling on her husband Mack. Mack and his partner, a puncher named Evins Baldwin, were roping some horses up on the Hashknife range when he got a couple of fingers caught in his dally. Mack examined the damage and found one finger missing and another hanging by a thread.

About that time Evins rode up, examined the wreck, and started belly laughing. When Mack asked what was so funny Evins pointed out that his dog Spot was eating the missing finger. Why, that potlicker didn't even have the good manners to carry it off, he just wagged his tail and ate the thing right in front of Mack. Evins didn't help matters either. He began expressing grave concern about whether Spot might get indigestion from eating human flesh.

Mack didn't have anything to use for a bandage except an old, used handkerchief he'd borrowed from Evins, so he used it to bind the wound. They made the long ride into Winslow to see if Doc Stump could save the other finger. On the way, Evins said sympathetically, "Damn, Mack, I sure hate it about ol' Spot eatin' your finger. He's the best ketch-dog I ever had, and I'd sure hate for his stomach to get upset eatin' human flesh." Then he slapped Mack on the leg and laughed until tears rolled down his cheek.

In Winslow, Doc distastefully removed the handkerchief, took one look at the finger and decided it had to come off. He cut off the finger and placed it in a tray. About that time, Doc's old angora tomcat, Romeo, suddenly awakened from his slumber behind a potbellied stove, leaped up on the table in a single bound, snatched the finger, and ran off with it, causing Evins and Doc Stump to break into laughter. "You'd be surprised," Doc said dryly, "at how many different cuts of meat that old cat gets in a day."

This story deserves at least a footnote in the cavalcade of Arizona history because it marks the first and perhaps only time a cowpuncher got to watch a potlickin' dog eat one finger and a tomcat eat the other—all in the same day!

CHAPTER 25

The Old Stadium

The old Stadium, located in downtown Scottsdale for so many years is now a part of history. Most of the fond reminiscences have centered around the major league teams who took spring training there over the past thirty-five years. My fondest memories, however, go back to the summer of 1956 when I was a wet-behind-the-ears, seventeen-year-old catcher for the Glendale Greys in the Valley Semi-Professional Baseball League.

We came to Scottsdale on a balmy Sunday afternoon in April to play the Scottsdale Blues in the brand new stadium. The stadium was nearly filled to capacity that day. The rye grass was new and the place still smelled of fresh paint. Among the Scottsdale players were local favorites Roy Coppinger, Bob Melton, and the Spradling brothers, Bob and Everett. But the real draw was a former minor league pitching sensation named Corky Reddell.

Remember, this was when baseball was really America's pastime. Professional basketball and football were small time in comparison. Golf and tennis were for the rich. Television was in the pioneer stage. Super Bowls, play-offs, and other televised sports spectaculars were light years away. The Dodgers were still in Brooklyn and the Giants were playing in the Polo Grounds. The biggest professional sport in Arizona in those days was Class C baseball—the colorful, old Arizona-Texas League.

Naturally, our sports heroes were local athletes and one of the biggest was Corky Reddell. Corky was a baseball legend due mostly to a fantastic season of 1953. That's when he won twenty-eight games for the Tucson Cowboys.

Now, I can't vouch for the veracity of this tale, but old-timers around Scottsdale tell the story of a scout for a big league team who came out to the Reddell farm east of town to try to sign Corky. Mr. Reddell told him Corky was out rabbit hunting and agreed to take the scout out to find him. When they found Corky, he was carrying a string of seven rabbits, but the scout can see no gun. Mr. Reddell explained that Corky always hunted with rocks, not bullets. And the scout is overjoyed to see that Corky throws left-handed. "That boy is just what we need," he declared, "a left-handed pitcher!"

But Mr. Reddell just shakes his head, refusing the scout's generous offer of a big contract. "I can't rightly accept your offer," he says, "it just wouldn't be honest. Y'see, Corky ain't left-handed. He just kills rabbits that-away. When he throws right-handed, he spoils the meat!"

Well, if that story isn't true, it should have been.

🌵 🌵 🌵

That reminds me of a time back in the early 1960s when I was playing banjo with a folk group. We were entertaining in a small honky-tonk in Mesa that was the favorite watering hole of the great 1930s ballplayer Charlie Grimm. Charlie was also a fine left-handed banjo player and used to sit in with us. At the time, Charlie was scouting for the Cubs. One night I was telling him about this great pitcher over in Scottsdale, named Jim Palmer. "Palmer is so good," I claimed, "I once watched him pitch seven innings in a driving rainstorm and he never got the ball wet!"

Charlie just gave me a skeptical look, so I continued. "Another time I saw him pitch fourteen innings and strike out every batter. Only one guy touched the ball and that was a lazy foul ball!"

Charlie's eyes brightened. "Marshall," he said, "let's go find that guy and sign him. The Cubs need hitters!"

🌵 🌵 🌵

Back to the great Reddell. Despite that great year when Corky won twenty-eight games for the Tucson Cowboys, he never rose higher in professional baseball. Rumor had it too much boozing and carousing had ended his professional career prematurely. I didn't know anything about that. Corky was one of my heroes, right up there with Mickey Mantle. I couldn't believe that on that sunny Sunday afternoon I was on the same playing field with the great Reddell. It mattered little to me that Corky had never made the big time, he was by far the most famous pitcher I'd ever seen up close.

The first time up I stepped in the box, dug in, and stared out at that figure glaring down at me from the mound. I was so awe-struck I took three called strikes. The same thing happened the second time up. I was determined, for the sake of my grandchildren, to at least get a foul ball off the great Reddell.

I didn't come up again until the sixth inning. By this time, Corky was looking pretty tired and disheveled. His blazing fastball was slowing up a bit. Perspiration rolled off his cheeks and onto his sweat-soaked uniform. He was several pounds over his playing weight and looked like he hadn't slept in days. I knew he wouldn't be in the game much longer and this might be my last chance to hit. I was determined to get on base somehow. I figured this late in the game he might not be too quick off the mound so on the first pitch I laid a bunt down the third base line and ran to first for all I was worth. I hit the bag just before I heard the pop of the ball hitting the glove. I stood on first, grinning at him and proud as a peacock.

"Counts the same as a line drive," I grinned. He dismissed my youthful, cocky impudence with a cold stare. I figured he'd stick one under my chin the next time up and was greatly relieved when he came out of the game in the next inning.

I never saw the great Reddell again. I heard he died a few years later, way before his time. I reckon it was the booze that got him. That was a real tragedy because he was a heck 'ov a great pitcher and could have gone all the way to the big show if things had been different.

The Glendale Greys went on to have a great season, losing in the state championship game to the Casa Grande Cotton Kings, the New York Yankees of the Arizona semi-pro league. I got lucky in the state tournament and hit over .400. I say lucky, because I didn't hit anywhere near that during the season. The papers made a big deal over a skinny, seventeen-year-old kid with a hot bat. That was quite a thrill, but it didn't come close to that day in the new Scottsdale Stadium when I got a *base hit* off the great Reddell.

🌵

CHAPTER 26

The Crazy Boatmen of Rio Salado

During World War II, the American military brass figured it would be smart to locate captured German seamen in prison camps as far away from water as possible. This made Arizona an ideal place. One of these camps was just north of the Salt River at Papago Park. With a logic that only a bureaucrat could understand, the army decided to locate all the incorrigible ones in one compound. The thought being that if they put all the hard core ones in one place they could keep them out of mischief. They should have asked a schoolteacher about that kind of logic. With all those criminal minds working together, an escape was as predictable as horseflies in July.

The Germans concocted a plan to tunnel out of the camp and make their way to Mexico, then back to the Fatherland. They got hold of a map that showed a rather large blue line just south of the camp. Normally, this signifies a river. The Salt River blue line joined another blue line known as the Gila River, which intersected with another blue line called the Colorado River, which ran into Mexico. A scheme was planned whereby they would tunnel out of the camp, then float down the rivers to Mexico. Three Germans went to work building a prefab boat which they planned to take with them through the tunnel and launch into the Salt. They were destined to become known as the "Crazy Boatmen."

What the Germans didn't know was that Arizona's rivers were normally dry, in fact the Salt had been waterless for years. Oblivious to the usual arid nature of Arizona's rivers, the determined P.O.W.s went on with their plans. They asked the camp commander for permission to build a volleyball court. He was happy to oblige with anything that would keep the boys out of mischief.

Next, they swiped spoons from the mess hall and began digging beneath one of the barracks. The dirt was mostly caliche, something akin to cement, but they dug on, filling their shorts and socks with dirt then ambling out for a round of volleyball. While jumping around, they scattered dirt from the diggings. They dug a hole 15 feet deep and 180 feet long.

On December 23, 1944, the greatest P.O.W. escape in the United States during World War II took place as twenty-five Germans headed for Mexico. Once on the outside, however, their well-thought-out plans went astray.

The weather turned cold and rainy. Two got discouraged and surrendered to a housewife. Another demoralized young seaman walked up to a farmhouse and gave himself up to a couple of children playing in the yard. The most disparaging event occurred when the three boatmen hauled their craft over to the Salt and prepared to launch. To this day in Germany, their comrades laughingly refer to them as the "Crazy Boatmen."

Most of the prisoners were caught soon after their escape. Their leader, Captain Jurgen Wattenberg, was the last to surrender. He was captured on January 28 in downtown Phoenix when he asked a gas station attendant for directions to the railroad station. His thick German accent gave him away. Wattenberg had hidden out in a cave not far from the famous Biltmore resort, lending credence to the claim that he was likely Arizona's first German winter visitor or "snowbird."

GRAHAM

CHAPTER 27

English is Not Outspoken Here

During Tombstone's heyday in the 1880s, the lure of riches attracted the wide gamut of frontier society from tinhorn gamblers to church deacons. Lawyers were among the first to arrive. Their offices were conveniently located between the courthouse on Toughnut Street and the bistros on Allen Street. Locals affectionately called the complex of law offices "Rotton Row."

Some of the most skilled attorneys in the West hung their shingles in Tombstone. None was more gifted than the irrepressible Allen English. He was an Eastern-educated attorney from an aristocratic Maryland family who found the practice of law in the East dull—too conventional for his venturesome spirit. So he headed out West for that "bibulous Babylon" of Tombstone.

The eccentric lawyer from Maryland cut a bodacious swath through Tombstone's rough-hewn society. He stood more than six feet tall and sported a magnificent crown of hair. Dressed in cutaway coat and striped pants, he moved with the grace of a ballet dancer. A skilled elocutionist, he could hold a jury spellbound with whispered emotion or with a voice ringing with resonance, he could launch a speech of fire and brimstone that would have done a preacher proud. People came from miles around to watch Tombstone's "courtroom colossus" in action. Clever and witty, he seduced many a jury by flattery, cajolery, crying, or begging. His rapier wit and unconventional antics kept spectators in hysterics, judges and opposing lawyers in a state of perturbation.

Allen English had at least two known vices—tobacco and ol' John Barleycorn. The former was of the chewing variety. He could spit with all the aplomb of a muleskinner. His admirers, and there were many, claimed he could spit over his shoulder and hit the inside of a cuspidor from ten feet. Folks naturally dubbed these, Allen's "Great Expectorations." Once he appeared in court hopelessly under the influence and was promptly fined $25 for contempt of court. Rising indignantly, he roared, "Your honor, that $25 wouldn't pay for half the contempt I have for this court."

Someone once called him outspoken. "He may be out-maneuvered, out-smarted, and out-thought," a weary prosecutor corrected, "but, sir, he is never out-spoken."

CHAPTER 28

The Man Who Killed Santa Claus

It was 1930 and the Great Depression was in full bloom. Hard times had fallen on the rural communities of Tempe and Mesa. It was also the height of the Christmas season and local merchants were feeling the pinch. Not only was business slack, but no one felt like celebrating. It looked as if the annual Christmas parade was going to be a big flop.

John McPhee, colorful editor of the *Mesa Tribune*, looked upon the dismal scenario and was determined to inject some spirit into the holidays. McPhee had more plans then a politician when it came to promotional schemes and he really outdid himself on this one. He came up with an idea that dazzled the town merchants with its brilliance.

"Why not," he suggested, "hire a parachutist to dress up in a Santa suit and jump from an airplane. Then he could lead the parade through town."

Never before, to anyone's knowledge, had anyone jumped from an airplane in a Santa suit. Keep in mind, parachuting was a dangerous stunt in 1930. In fact, aviation was still in its infancy. Lindbergh had crossed the Atlantic solo only three years before.

Even the most skeptical merchants agreed. McPhee's plan was sure to attract spectators and they, in turn, would spend money. Their eyes sparkled in gleeful anticipation. They could already hear the jingle bells of their cash registers ringing up sales.

McPhee hired an itinerant stunt pilot to don the Santa suit and make the parachute jump. Everything went according to plan until the morning of the event when Santa failed to appear. A large crowd was already gathering as the editor searched frantically for the missing Santa. McPhee finally found his man at a local saloon screwing up his courage. He was so drunk he couldn't hit the floor with his stocking cap in five tries.

"Fear not!" the irrepressible McPhee told the worried merchants. "I'll borrow a department store dummy, dress him in the Santa suit. The pilot can push him out. Then I'll appear in another Santa suit and nobody will know the difference."

The merchants were skeptical but no one could come up with a better idea so the department store dummy in the Santa suit was loaded aboard the biplane and off they flew into the wild blue yonder.

The crowd peered anxiously skyward as the little biplane circled overhead. The merchants stood by their cash registers awaiting the rush of business that was sure to follow on the footsteps of McPhee's ingenious idea.

Suddenly, the door to the airplane opened and there stood Santa in the opening. The crowd let out a cheer. Then Santa leaped, or rather was shoved out the door and tumbled end over end towards the ground.

Down,

Down,

Down, came the department store dummy in the rented Santa suit.

Splat! Santa hit the ground unceremoniously on the edge of a field in full view of hundreds of horrified spectators.

McPhee was undaunted by the sudden turn of events. He emerged in his own Santa suit waving to the crowd as if nothing unusual had occurred.

But the crowd wasn't buying. Parents gathered up their dazed children and headed for home. Merchants gazed around their empty stores in dismay. McPhee was about as welcome as a coyote in a henhouse.

John McPhee left town for a few days, hoping that all would be soon forgotten, but it wasn't. He would always be remembered as "the man who killed Santa Claus."

CHAPTER 29

The Day Patrick Murphy Bombed Naco

Patrick Murphy was one of those hellbent-for-leather barnstorming pilots back when flying was still a novelty. He'd fly into some town or rural area and put on a show of aerial stunts. He'd also make a few extra bucks taking folks up for a ride in his flying machine.

During the Mexican Revolution, which began in 1910 and lasted off and on until 1929, American adventurers, and that included barnstorming pilots, found they could make big bucks by selling their unique talents. And the Mexicans usually paid off in gold. Some of the earliest combat in aviation history occurred near the Arizona-Mexican border.

In 1911, Hector Worden was hired by Francisco Madero's revolutionaries to fly missions against the *federales*. Two years later, Didier Masson attacked a federale gunboat off Guaymas using homemade bombs of pipe filled with dynamite.

He'd make a low run at the target, light the fuse, and hurl it in the general direction of the craft. Masson didn't hit the gunboat, but did succeed in causing the frightened sailors to abandon ship and paddle frantically for shore.

Pancho Villa was also quick to see the advantage of using airplanes for combat. He wanted his own air force, so hired an American stunt pilot named Ed Parsons to train his cadets. Villa had no air field so training began in a cow pasture. Villa's air cadets were all lined up alongside the landing strip to watch Parsons demonstrate landing techniques. The landing was particularly rough and the plane wound up with its nose in the dirt and its tail in the air. When the smoke and dust had cleared, all of Villa's cadets had lit out. One might say Pancho Villa's Air Force project never got off the ground.

🌵 🌵 🌵

During the 1929 revolution, Patrick Murphy signed on with the revolutionaries to bomb the *federale* trenches around Naco, Sonora. There are two Nacos, one in Arizona, the other in Sonora. The fighting along the border attracted a number of spectators from towns like Bisbee and Douglas. Folks watched the battles around Agua Prieta from ringside seats atop the Gadsden Hotel in Douglas. Over at Naco, railroad cars were pulled alongside the border so the residents of nearby Bisbee would have good seats. Battles were usually fought during daylight hours, thus providing ample time for the combatants on both sides to sample the night life in Naco, Sonora.

The *federales* were entrenched on three sides around Naco and since the fourth side was the town of Naco, Arizona, the rebels were in a predicament. So Patrick

Murphy was sent out to bomb the defenders. Bombing runs were more sophisticated by 1929. The pilot was no longer required to fly the plane and throw out the bombs. A Mexican youth sat in the second seat and he lit the fuse, usually with a cigarette, and tossed the bomb overboard.

Patrick Murphy took off that morning and circled the *federale* trenches. What happened next remains a mystery to this day. For reasons known only to himself, Murphy turned his biplane towards Naco, Arizona and made a bombing run at the local Phelps Dodge Mercantile Store. The drama took on a comic opera atmosphere as Murphy circled and made ready for another run. Some sharp-shooter stepped outside with a hunting rifle and shot Murphy down. He crash landed outside of Naco and was hauled off to jail in Nogales. The United States was trying to stay out of the fracas and took a dim view of any of its citizens selling their services to either side.

Before anybody could get Patrick Murphy's rendition of the story, he flew the coop and seems to have disappeared, as they say, from the pages of history. Murphy's bombardment of Naco is claimed to be the only time the continental United States has ever been bombed from an airplane by a "foreign power."

CHAPTER 30

Frontier Passports

Back in the early days, when only a few brave daring men ventured into the wilderness, the dangers were many. Freezing winters, searing deserts, grizzly bears and unfriendly natives all took their toll. In 1856, Antoine Robidoux could account for only three survivors out of some 300 whom he'd known in the Rockies thirty years earlier. James O. Pattie noted that out of 160 trappers in the Gila country, only sixteen survived a single season.

As time went by and the minority became the vast majority, it was the Indian who became the endangered one. The newcomers, out of fear or for a variety of reasons, believed the only good Indian was a dead Indian. Innocent ones were sometimes shot on sight, their only crime was venturing too near a white encampment.

In an effort to protect friendly Indians, early military expeditions in the Southwest presented official-looking documents for safe passage among whites. The testimonial attested to the fact that the bearer was a man of good character and should be treated accordingly. A red ribbon and seal was attached, which greatly pleased the natives.

Occasionally, a belligerent war chief would demand one, most likely to gain easy access to somebody's camp. In an effort to avoid trouble, the officers usually complied. They presented the rogue the same document but wrote: "This fellow is an untrustworthy scalawag. Don't trust him out of your sight." One can imagine the results when the rascal rode into some camp and proudly presented his "safe passage."

🌵 🌵 🌵

In the Bradshaw Mountains of Arizona, an old trapper named Paulino Weaver came up with his own plan and, for a time, succeeded. Paulino, whose real name was Powell (he acquired Paulino from his Hispanic friends), was part Indian and understood their dilemma better than anyone in the Gila country.

When whites and Indians met on a friendly basis in the mountains, they invariably enjoyed a smoke together. The word "tobacco" was a byword in the wilderness. Paulino devised a plan whereby the friendly Indians would call out "Paulino-tobacco" whenever they encountered a party of whites. Because there were few whites at the time, and all knew Paulino, the plan worked wonderfully, but it was eventually doomed to failure. After the Arizona country was overrun with argonauts, the newcomers either didn't know of the great mountain man or didn't care. But, for a time, "Paulino-tobacco" meant safe passage in the wild country.

🌵 🌵 🌵

Later, Weaver himself became a victim of the animosity between the newcomers and the natives. One day, while out alone, he was attacked by a hostile war party. He took a bullet in a vital spot and, believing himself mortally wounded, began his "death song," a warrior ritual he'd adopted from the Plains Indians, but unknown among the Yavapai bands. Out on the Plains, enemy warriors waited respectfully while a fallen foe went through the ritual before administering the *coup de grace.* In this instance, the Yavapai warriors thought Weaver had gone loco and refused to go near him.

Sometime later, Weaver realized he wasn't going to die, not yet anyway, so he got up and walked back to his camp. The Yavapai apparently regretted shooting their old friend because during the next few months, they continually sent out inquiries about his health as the old man recovered from his wounds.

CHAPTER 31

First Class Train Ride

Back in the latter part of the 19th century, in the mountains of eastern Arizona, an entrepreneur named Del Potter ran a little railroad he proudly named the Clifton and Northern. The line ran from the little town of Clifton to a mine north of town so the name seemed to fit. The Clifton and Northern railroad had only one engine and that was pulled by a mule, but Del considered himself a full-fledged president of a railroad with all privileges and courtesies.

Railroad companies, by custom, issued passes to owners and presidents of other lines. Thus, railroad nabobs were allowed free passage to travel anywhere in the country on other lines. Potter saw this as an opportunity to see the country first class. He printed up elaborate passes for his Clifton and Northern Railroad and sent them out to all the railroad presidents in the country. They reciprocated and soon Del had enough passes to take an extended vacation. He closed down his line and hit the road, seeing the country first class.

Everywhere he traveled, Potter was treated with the proper respect generally accorded the president of a railroad. He slept in the comfortable pullman cars and feasted in the fancy dining cars.

Del Potter might have gone on traveling indefinitely had not one of his fellow-presidents, a man who prided himself on having ridden on every railroad in America, decided to take a ride on the Clifton and Northern line. To get to the town of Clifton was quite an ordeal in itself. The nearest real railroad terminated at La Junta, Colorado, some 700 miles away. The rest of the journey was a long, arduous wagon ride across some of the roughest country in the West. When the exasperated railroad president finally reached Clifton and got a first hand look at the Clifton and Northern line with its mule-powered railroad, he indignantly decided to forego the ride and returned in a huff to his eastern home.

It wasn't long before Potter received notification that he had been unceremoniously expelled from the distinguished and select fraternity of railroad presidents.

CHAPTER 32

Lost Mines in Convenient Places

Have you ever wondered why most of our fabled lost mines are located close to large cities or along major highways? It's probably for the same reason that great events always occur next door to museums.

Modern day argonauts prefer convenience. It's always nice to come home to a cold beer and a soft bed after a hard day searching for some elusive *madre del oro*. More than a few old windjammers claimed to have been able to see the fabled Lost Dutchman from the back porch of their suburban homes on the outskirts of Phoenix. I reckon just knowing it's out there somewhere is satisfaction enough.

Kearney Egerton called lost mines our greatest natural resources. They don't pollute the sky with columns of acrid smoke, collect garbage, befoul streams, or scar the delicate hillsides with unsightly tailings. And they don't cost the taxpayers a cent to maintain and equip—no asphalt parking lots, restrooms, or visitor centers. Lost mines are just good, clean, cheap fun. And, for the *True Believer*, they are as real as a mermaid to a lonesome sailor or a kettle full of gold at the rainbow's end.

ψ ψ ψ

Two of our lesser-known lost mines are so close to major highways you hardly have to leave your vehicle to get to the treasure.

On State Route 87, between Payson and Phoenix, is Mount Ord. On the eastern side of the mountain, are the ruins of old Camp Reno. Back in the 1860s, Indians used to purchase goods at the military post with gold they mined in the nearby Mazatzal Mountains. One day, five would-be millionaires decided to follow the natives into the rugged mountains and find their horde of gold. The goldseekers vanished without a trace. Five years later, their sunbleached skeletons were found on the north side of Mount Ord. Scattered among the bones were chunks of quartzs glittering with—you guessed it—pure gold.

Another fabulous treasure lies within rock-throwing distance of Interstate 17. During the 1870s, a couple of idle prospectors in Phoenix observed an Indian buying supplies with gold nuggets. They decided to follow him through the desert and into the mountains north of town along a path that is today Interstate 17.

Somewhere in the vicinity of today's Black Canyon City, they lost the Indian's trail but found what they were searching for—granite boulders laced with gold. They loaded their saddlebags with rich specimens, memorized the surroundings and, just to make sure, drove a prospector's pick into one of the golden boulders. Vowing to return to collect the rest of the treasure, they mounted up and rode out.

They hadn't ridden far when they were bushwhacked by Indians who resented having their pockets of gold picked by these unwanted interlopers. One of the pair got away and didn't stop running until he reached California. Several years later he returned but—you guessed it again—couldn't find the so-called Lost Pick Mine. And neither has anyone else.

ψ ψ ψ

Up near Sycamore Canyon there lived a cattleman who didn't trust banks so he cached his money in post holes around the ranch. It was a good place to hide it since once the posts were put back in place there was no evidence left behind. Only problem was, he died without telling the rest of his family beneath which posts the money was buried. They spent years going around the place digging up fence posts and never did find their inheritance. It's still buried out there—somewhere.

ψ ψ ψ

Walnut Grove Dam, on the Hassayampa River, had just been built and a three-mile-long lake had formed behind it when heavy rains came in late February of 1891. Dan Burke was sent downstream to warn the people of the pending disaster. This Arizona-style Paul Revere decided to stop at Bob Brow's saloon and have a drink. Then he paid a visit to one of the ladies upstairs. By the time he was ready to resume his infamous ride the dam burst and sent a 110-foot-high tidal wave down the Hassayampa River past Bob Brow's saloon taking a safe full of gold with it.

To this day, searchers meander up and down the usually-dry Hassayampa, an Indian word meaning "river that flows upside down," hoping the shifting sands might have uncovered the safe. Brow, who later owned the Palace Bar in Prescott, was able to recoup his losses by regaling his customers with tales of where the safe may have settled. The saloonkeeper could stretch his windies out to last ten shots of whiskey at two bits a shot.

ψ ψ ψ

Old-timers swore the Lost Belle McKeever was the richest gold strike ever discovered in North America. The legend began in 1869 when a war party of Yavapai attacked the McKeever family as their wagon was fording the river at Gila Bend. Most of the family was massacred in the attack and a young girl, Belle, was taken captive by the braves. A brother, Abner, had been on the opposite side of the river when the attack came and witnessed his sister's abduction.

Three soldiers from Fort Yuma were dispatched to find Belle, but the searing desert heat was so intense that two of their horses died of thirst, leaving them afoot. The next day one of the soldiers suffered from sunstroke and went insane. The following day the soldiers stumbled upon a small stream and, as they knelt down for a drink, spotted gold nuggets, "big as buckshot." They had no idea where they were except that it was somewhere in the vicinity of the Harquahala Mountains. They panned with coffee cups and dug out ten pounds of gold in a few minutes. But, after getting dysentery from eating raw horsemeat, they decided to try to find their way out.

They marked the site and named it the Belle McKeever, in honor of the young lady they were searching for and, with fifty pounds of gold in their saddlebags, headed for Fort Yuma. On the way out, one died and another had gone crazy from the heat. The lone survivor, a man named Flanigan, tried many times to retrace his path to the gold but came up empty. Poor Belle McKeever remained as lost as the mine named for her.

ψ ψ ψ

Somewhere out there, near the highway from Phoenix to Parker, lies the mislaid Lost Six Shooter. That one began in 1884 when P. J. Jenkins, superintendent of the Planet Mine, was lost in a blinding sandstorm on his way back to Planet Town, on the Bill Williams River, from Tyson Wells. Tyson Wells is known today as Quartzsite.

Jenkins sought shelter from the storm among some rocks. While waiting for the winds to quit, he spotted a magnificent ledge of gold right before his eyes! He quickly broke off some samples and stuffed them in his holster, then left his six-shooter on the rocks as a marker. He then set out for Planet Town. Two days later his horse arrived home with an empty saddle. A search party went out and found his body lying half buried in a sandy arroyo. Before dying, Jenkins had scribbled a message saying: "Found gold ledge by rocks fifteen feet high. Two rocks look alike. Knocked off some pieces. Very rich. Dust in air too thick to tell exact location. Think it is above ravine I come up seven miles."

The samples in Jenkins' holster assayed out at $25,000 to the ton. There were other gold strikes in the area, but none have fit P. J. Jenkins' description.

Next time you're traveling down those Arizona highways, you *True Believers*, keep your eyes peeled. The gold's out there . . . somewhere.

ψ

CHAPTER 33

Bear Facts on the History of Christopher Creek

Few people get a chance to attend their own funeral—alive that is. But Isadore Christopher did. He is likely one of the few in Arizona history who was a live witness to his own funeral. It all happened back in the 1880s up in the Mogollon Rim country where Christopher had a small ranch located on the creek named for him.

While riding one day, he came upon a large bear. He shot the critter, then hauled it back to the ranch and dumped it in a log shanty. Later that day, he rode out to gather some cattle and, while he was away, a war party of Apaches decided to pay a social call. Finding nobody at home, they set fire to Christopher's humble abodes.

A troop of cavalry arrived at the ranch a few minutes after the Apaches had vamoosed. The soldiers inspected the smoldering ruins and found some cooked remains. They naturally figured it was pore ol' Isadore Christopher and decided he needed a proper burial.

A grave was hastily dug and funeral services were begun. During the ceremony, Christopher casually rode in, quickly sized up the situation, and informed the solemn party they were holding a funeral for the carcass of an old bear.

CHAPTER 34

A Sure Way to Get Elected

George Ruffner was Yavapai County's perennial sheriff, serving more terms than any other in Arizona history. He was a topnotch peace officer; he could track bees in a blizzard, and nearly always "got his man." Ruffner liked being sheriff but he hated having to campaign for political office. He was an old cowboy at heart and was uncomfortable having to stand on a platform with a bunch of office seekers and make long-winded political speeches.

Sheriff Ruffner had lots of admirers, but his most ardent fan was Sandy Huntington. Sandy had been exiled to Prescott by his illustrious relatives in California for excessive imbibing. He was an intelligent, likable fellow who made friends easily around Yavapai County. When he was sober, which wasn't often, Sandy hung around Ruffner's livery stable digging post holes, cleaning corrals, and doing odd jobs.

Old-timers claim Sandy was the one who dreamed up the creative financing plan used at Ruffner's stables for boarding horses. In plan A, for $5 a day you could board your horse and Sandy would sweep out the stall. Plan B only cost $3.50 a day but you had to sweep out the stall. Plan C cost 50 cents a day. Who sweeps? There ain't nothin' to sweep.

🌵   🌵   🌵

One particular election year, lots of folks, including Sandy, feared George might lose because he stubbornly refused to campaign. Thus, Sandy was inspired to take matters in his own hands.

Because there were so many illiterate voters in those days, the county always provided someone to read and mark the ballot for those who couldn't. Sandy volunteered his services. He stood next to the ballot box and offered free advice to voters who couldn't make up their minds.

When a voter announced he couldn't read, Sandy would read the list of the candidates and mark the ballot according to the voter's wishes. When they came to the office of sheriff, Sandy would give the two candidates names. If the voter said, "George Ruffner," Sandy would take a pen and deliberately mark an X in the square next to George's name.

Not everyone shared Sandy's devotion to Sheriff Ruffner. "I ain't votin' for that damn Ruffner," one voter scoffed. Obligingly, Sandy took the ballot and, with great aplomb, placed a big X in the square next to George Ruffner's name saying, "Then we'll just cross out that ol' son-of-a-gun." And cheerfully dropped the ballot in the box.

🌵

CHAPTER 35

The Original
Neighborhood Activist

Earl Goodrich loved sitting on the front porch of his Cave Creek home in the beautiful, unspoiled Sonoran Desert. Cars were seldom seen on the narrow, unpaved road in front of his house. That all seemed likely to change one day when a couple of county surveyors strolled into what he'd always thought was his front yard and started pounding stakes in the ground.

His curiosity was aroused sufficiently to ask what they were doing. "We're marking out a new street," one cheerfully replied.

Earl didn't say anything, but as soon as they were gone, he went out to the shed and got out his shovel and wheelbarrow. He loaded the wheelbarrow with rocks and dumped them out between the rows of stakes.

When he had enough rocks, Earl shaped them into a mound about six feet long and nailed two boards together in the shape of a cross and drove it into the ground. Then he reached into his pocket, took out a pocket-knife, and on the crossboard scrawled the words, "Buck Skinner, 1879-1947, Rest In Peace."

Earl sat on his porch and waited patiently for something to happen and sure enough, a few weeks later, a crew with some heavy equipment showed up. Before they could get their engines cranked up, Earl ran up with the look of a true concerned citizen and informed the county men they were about to disturb the remains of one of the pioneer pillars of the community, a stalwart Arizonan who helped tame this wilderness land.

"And, if you don't believe me," he said with poker-faced honesty, "go over to Harold's Cave Creek Corral and ask Harold and Ruth Gavagan." Harold and Ruth ran a popular steakhouse in Cave Creek and had lived in the area longer than most of the saguaros. Black Mountain was just an anthill when those two came to town and no one doubted their knowledge of local history.

Sure enough, straight-faced Harold and Ruth Gavagan verified Earl's story. A few days later, some officials from the county came out and looked over the burial site. With serious expressions of grave concern (no pun intended), they climbed back in their cars and left without saying a word.

Sometime later, the surveyors were back in the area mapping out a new street, where a road was eventually built, this one a half mile from Earl's house. That was many years ago and Earl still sits out on his front porch every evening enjoying the undisturbed view of the beautiful high desert.

PART FOUR

The Gentle Tamers

CHAPTER 36

The Saga of Pearl Hart and Joe Boot

One day in 1899, Pearl Hart and Joe Boot decided to up their station in life by robbing a stagecoach. Unlike real outlaws of the West, the pair didn't have any horses to make their getaway and had only one six-shooter between them.

Undaunted, Pearl and Joe made their heist near the town of Kelvin on the Gila River as the stage was making its run from Tucson to Globe. Pearl made up for the shortage of firearms by swiping the stage driver's pistol. Since the two were afoot, a posse quickly gathered in the two pedestrians.

Rough-hewn Pearl had pulled the robbery dressed in baggy men's clothes, but appeared for trial dressed up like a schoolmarm on her way to a church social. On the witness stand, Pearl was a Western Sarah Bernhardt, playing every role from consummate coquette to repentant sinner. In a sweet voice, Pearl informed the jurors she was such a proper lady she wouldn't even stay in the same room with a clock that was fast. During her school days, she'd refused to do improper fractions.

She flirted with the all-male jury continuously throughout the proceedings, occasionally lifted her skirts and crossed her legs, revealing a pair of shapely ankles. The jury proceeded to find Joe Boot guilty and Pearl *innocent.*

The judge was outraged, insisted that Pearl be retried, this time for stealing the stage driver's gun and tampering with the U.S. mail (not male) This time she was sentenced to a term in the Yuma Territorial Prison, the infamous "Hell Hole."

During the trial, the Eastern press had romanticized Pearl to the point of believing that she had robbed the stage in order to get money to visit her ailing mother back East somewhere. Despite the fact that Pearl had a rather checkered past, the press was appalled that the beautiful, virtuous "girl bandit" was being hauled off to prison by those uncurried scoundrels out in Arizona.

For her part, Pearl enjoyed the notoriety and played it to the hilt. Finally, after the hoopla died down, she requested an audience with the warden and informed him that she was expecting a baby. Naturally, the warden was troubled by this revelation, mainly because only two men had spent any time alone with Pearl—he and the territorial governor.

After an exchange of telegrams, it was decided to parole Pearl on the condition that she leave the territory. She was most eager to oblige.

Pearl Hart headed back East, capitalizing on her fame by giving lectures, comparable today to hitting the talk show circuit. She also reenacted her daring stage robbery on stage. Written into the story was a fictional part about needing money to visit her sick mother.

Pearl also fictionalized her pregnancy. The fertile-minded "girl bandit" wasn't pregnant, it just seemed like a good way to get out of prison. In those days, men took a woman at her word when it concerned such delicate matters.

CHAPTER 37

The Belles of Boomtown

Female performers who played in the rough-hewn mining camp theaters had an edge on their male counterparts simply because they were women. That alone was enough, in many parts of the West, to draw a crowd. Actresses then, as now, were the harbingers of social change.

Lotta Crabtree, appearing on stage while still a teenager, shocked audiences by baring her legs and smoking on stage. Lotta, a strikingly beautiful lady, with sparkling eyes and lustrous blond hair, was America's highest paid actress during her heyday. Talented performers could attract high prices. Tickets to see Lola Montez in San Francisco during the 1860s cost $65 apiece. Provocative encores could be lucrative, too.

Adah Issacs Menken appeared in *La Mezappa* in Virginia City, Nevada, in a role that called for her to ride across the stage strapped to the back of a horse wearing nothing but a transparent, flesh-colored body stocking (Adah, not the horse). The mostly male audience was so inspired by the illusion of this beautiful, nude nymph strapped to a black stallion that when Adah came out for an encore, they began throwing money on the stage. Adah knew a good deal when she saw it. Wearing nothing but a smile and a gauzy body stocking, she made encore after encore, raking in thousands of dollars in gratuities from her lusty, red-blooded male admirers.

One cowboy was so taken by a show business belle singing the sentimental ballad, "The Last Kiss My Darling Mother Gave," he threw her a $20 gold piece. She reached up to snatch it but missed and the coin conked her on the noggin, knocking the poor girl senseless.

But there were limits to what these lonely men would tolerate. A young lady name Antoinette Adams climbed on a stage in Virginia City one night and began to warble. She was described as ugly enough to make a peeping tom pull down her shade, and her singing sounded like a burro with a bad cold.

After listening politely to Miss Adams' opening number, a miner got up and proposed a collection be taken up so that she might be granted a well-deserved and immediate retirement from show business. The customers all made generous contributions.

When a traveling troupe that featured a well-known singer came to Prescott, a cowboy bought a ticket, then tried to talk his partner into going along. "Is she any good?" his friend inquired.

"Good? Why she's a virtuoso," the cowboy boasted.

"I don't care about her morals," he declared. "I want to know if she can sing."

Occasionally performers fell on hard times, even in the rich boom towns. One time in Tombstone, an acting troupe couldn't pay their hotel bill so the town marshal impounded their trunks, thus leaving the ladies with nothing to wear but costume leotards. After a few shows in the hot, sweaty theater without a change of clothes, the citizens demanded the marshal relinquish their trunks so the ladies could get some fresh clothing.

The combination of unsophisticated audiences and good acting sometimes created a few surprises. One evening in Tombstone, an old prospector sat silently through a melodrama watching the cold-hearted landlord order a poor widow out of her home because she couldn't pay the rent.

The sourdough was so moved by her pleas for pity that he walked up and tossed his gold-filled poke sack onto the stage. He broke up both the actors and the audience when, with tears streaming down his cheeks, he said, "Here, take this and pay off the old s.o.b." Sentimental old prospectors weren't the only ones to reveal a lack of sophistication in the theater.

One night in Tombstone's Bird Cage Theater, a traveling troupe was performing *Uncle Tom's Cabin* for the locals. During the dramatic scene when the dogs were chasing poor little Eliza, a drunken cowboy got caught up in the drama and drew his six-shooter and shot the dog. Next day the cowboy, now sober and sorry, offered his horse as recompense.

Another time, the beautiful female lead in a play became ill just before a performance and a local prostitute was persuaded to fill in for the evening. The third act called for the lady to die tragically, murdered by a jealous lover. After committing the dastardly deed, the actor faced the audience and in great remorse cried,

"What have I done? What have I done?"

A cowboy in the audience stood up and shouted, "I'll tell you what you've done. You've just killed the best whore in Tombstone!"

CHAPTER 38

Saturday Night Baths

Down in Cochise County, near Dos Cabezas, there used to be a mining operation known as the Mascot and Western Mining Company. Back around the turn of the century, during hard economic times, the headquarters in New York City decided to move its entire office staff to the Mascot. The group of transfers included twenty-eight female secretaries, whose idea of the Far West was Indiana. Few had ever been west of Hoboken, New Jersey.

The ladies' arrival in Mascot caused quite a stir, as women were about as scarce as Republicans around mining camps in those days. A bunch of local, love-starved cowboys formed a welcoming committee and took it upon themselves to throw a Saturday night dance to welcome the new arrivals. On the evening of the festivity, those Eastern ladies did what they normally did prior to going out back East—they all took baths. Nobody thought to tell them that the town had a limited water supply.

The dance went well, everybody had a good time, and couldn't wait to do it all over again. Until the next day, when somebody discovered that the town had gone dry. Even the mine had to shut down operations until the holding tanks could be refilled.

The sympathetic editor of the local newspaper discussed the dilemma saying:

"It is understood that there is an opening here for some efficiency engineer that can figure out a plan to provide baths for the stenographers and supply enough water to keep the mine going at the same time. The problem is most serious on Saturday nights. At this particular property, it is more important to keep the stenographers in good operating condition than the mines."

CHAPTER 39

Sometimes They Really Did Ride Off into the Sunset Together

Dime novels were staples for connoisseurs of adventure reading during the last century. Frank Starr's Ten-Cent Pocket Library and the dime novels of Beadle and Adams regaled hair-raising tales and legendary feats of men like Kit Carson and Buffalo Bill Cody. Not as well known among aficionados today were heroines like Hurricane Nell, Bess the Trapper, and Mountain Kate. These ladies roped, rode, shot, and fought their way through countless romantic adventures. All were permitted to be violent in defense of their virtue.

Keeping with Victorian tradition of the times, however, they always remained ladies. The outfits they wore were surprisingly sexy for the times. Nell wore a tight-fitting buckskin outfit that proudly displayed her ample curves. Bess wrapped herself in an Indian blanket. What she had on between her and the blanket was left to the imagination. And Kate wore a bleached dress made of soft doeskin.

Like their male counterparts, these fictional ladies had legions of fans and admirers in the East. Unlike the male heroes, who usually rode off into the sunset, still unhitched, the ladies usually wound up getting married to some wealthy, but mundane, doctor, lawyer, or banker and settling down back East.

※　※　※

Mary Taylor qualifies as a real-life dime novel heroine. She rode into Gila Bend in 1869, with a party of emigrants bound for California. She was traveling with a man named Nash, to whom she wasn't married; however, her fellow travelers discretely referred to as "Mrs. Nash." Apparently, she and Nash weren't hitting it off too well, for she had written in her journal: "I was tard of the trip, my husban' and I had been fussin'." Mary might have gone on to a dreary life in California had fate not intervened in the person of a tall, handsome stranger on horseback.

At Gila Bend, she met a dark, rugged-looking man named King Woolsey. Mary didn't know it at the time, but Woolsey was one of Arizona's most prominent citizens. He was not only a member of the territorial legislature, but he was also a tough, hardbitten leader of several civilian Indian fighting expeditions.

The courtship was brief, Woolsey didn't even take the time to get down off his horse. After a few words, Mary climbed up behind him and the two rode off into the sunset. During her years with Woolsey, Mary had a number of adventures. Once, she single-handedly captured a notorious outlaw.

When Woolsey died, she married a man named Taylor, and outlived him, too. Mary was a natural businesswoman investing heavily in ranches and real estate. She amassed a fortune of over two million dollars and, when she died in 1928, the Arizona state flags flew at half-mast.

CHAPTER 40

Mother Maggard
Saves the Day

By custom, Indian warriors spent a good deal of time preparing for battle. Much concern was given to ritual. They usually understood the strengths and weaknesses of their adversaries and made plans accordingly. Naturally, with such best-laid plans, something out of the ordinary was going to give them cause for consternation. Such was the case with Mother Maggard's wagon train.

Soon after a prospector's pick uncovered the first gold nugget in the foothills where Denver now stands, wagon trains filled with settlers, dreamers, schemers, and goldseekers crossed the Great Plains, bound for the gold-laden Rockies. Advertisements by merchants and land dealers painted a rosy picture of untold riches being uncovered daily.

Their advertisements were so convincing that one greenhorn was seen leaving Independence, Missouri, heading for Colorado, wearing a fancy suit, top hat, and spats. He was pushing a wheelbarrow. Someone asked what the wheelbarrow was for and he replied it was for the gold. He was going to load up his wheelbarrow with the yellow metal and push it back to Missouri.

Promoters neglected to warn the would-be million-aires of the dangers in crossing the hundreds of miles of endless plains. There were no towns or villages. There weren't even any facilities or campgrounds along the way. If fact, they were crossing Indian lands and the natives were downright resentful of the trespassers. War parties attacked the wagon trains on a regular basis.

🌵 🌵 🌵

A grey-haired old widow woman known unaffection-ately as Mother Maggard was a member of one of these emigrant parties bound for Colorado. She wore her silver hair in a severe bun and, on first impression, seemed to be a mean old hag. Beneath that tough exterior, however, was an even tougher interior. Most of the folks gave her a wide berth and cut her plenty of slack. If Mother Maggard had a weakness, it was for children. They feared her stern countenance, at first, but soon began to congregate around her wagon at night where she regaled them with ghostly campfire stories. She wore store-bought teeth and sometimes during the scariest part of a story she would push her false teeth outside her mouth and snarl at the youngsters. They screamed in mock hor-ror, loving every terrifying moment.

One day, somewhere out in eastern Colorado, a large war party of Arapaho swarmed down from their lair and attacked the wagon train. The wagonmaster circled the wagons and the men grabbed their guns and prepared for the desperate struggle that was sure to follow. The warriors punctuated the air with fierce war cries and rode hellbent-for-leather towards the train, stirring great clouds of dust. Both sides opened fire and the acrid smell of smoke filled the air. For what seemed like an eternity, there was noise and confusion that always accompanies battle. Then the Indians withdrew to rendezvous and plan their next attack. The situation in the wagon train was fast becoming desperate. Ammunition was running low. They couldn't withstand another attack. Men cast a worried look towards their families and women clutched their children.

The war chiefs signaled with their lances and the braves launched a series of fierce, blood-curdling yells and charged again. As they rode in this time, a strange thing happened, causing them to pause in astonishment a few hundred yards from the train. Standing atop the seat of one of the wagons was Mother Maggard. She was calling attention to herself by waving a skillet and shriek-ing madly. Her shrill, screeching voice was every bit as terrifying as the war cries of the Indians.

The apprehensive braves rode in for a closer look and, when they did, Mother Maggard waved her skillet and shrieked again. Only this time, the female paleface was snapping her false teeth at the startled braves from a position outside her mouth. Now, they'd never seen a pair of store-bought teeth. The unusual sight of this shrieking, grey-haired old harridan with snapping teeth located outside her mouth was more than those poor fellows could take. Their medicine didn't cover this bi-zarre situation. The war chiefs made a quick decision to withdraw from battle and let the strange lady warrior and her band pass.

Thus, Mother Maggard gloriously rode the rest of the way to Denver in a place of honor at the head of the grateful wagon train.

CHAPTER 41

Nellie's Navy

Most folks are well-aware of the occasional sibling rivalry between Arizona and California. It's been going on for quite some time. It began back in the 1850s when the vigilance committees around San Francisco gathered up most of their nefarious reprobates and gave them a choice of being hung or moving to Arizona. The meanest ones opted for the latter. The rivalry continued when goldseekers and other would-be millionaires arrived a decade later, wresting the precious gold from Arizona's mineral-laden hills and hauling it back to California.

The granddaddy of all issues, however, was water. Arizonans have always been quick to fight over their water rights. Senator Barry Goldwater made that clear during the 1970s when President Jimmy Carter wanted to cut back on some government funded water projects. "Mr. President," he said, "there's three things a Westerner will fight over—water, women, and gold—in that order."

It was water that nearly caused a shooting war in 1934 between the states of Arizona and California. At least the Arizonans were ready to draw their six-shooters. Trouble started when a California utilities company started construction on a large diversion dam on the Colorado River. The Arizonans, normally a temperate, mild-mannered breed, were outraged to learn that the water stored behind that dam would be used solely by Californians. What really put a burr under the saddle blankets of Arizonans was the fact that California was the only state using the water that didn't *contribute* any water to the river. Governor Ben Moeur, a crusty country doctor, was so infuriated by California's power-play politics he ordered the Arizona National Guard to the border.

At Parker, the soldiers became acquainted with a colorful lady riverboat pilot named Nellie T. Bush. She was proprietor of two small steamboats, the *Nellie T.* and the *Julia B.*, which she graciously consented to loan the guardsmen.

One dark night, the two little paddlewheelers, flying the Arizona flag, set out to reconnoiter the enemy shores of California. The Arizonans had little experience around water. Most of them had never seen a river that actually had water in it. During the confusion, the boats got entangled in some steel cables and, much to their red-faced chagrin, the desert sailors had to be rescued by the Californians.

Newspapers all over the country picked up on the story, making much ado about the "Arizona Navy" and its "battleships." Sometimes, even in defeat, one salvages everlasting glory. For her patriotic services to the state, Governor Moeur commissioned Nellie Bush, the first and only "Admiral of the Arizona Navy."

Later that year, the Californians began construction on a trestle bridge across the river that would "touch the sacred soil of Arizona," something that caused Doc Moeur to declare martial law. Much to the delight of some sabre-rattling Arizonans, he ordered the guardsmen to set up machine gun nests on the high cliffs overlooking the dam. The guns were trained on the construction workers, causing an immediate work stoppage. At this point, the U.S. Supreme Court got into the act and ordered Governor Moeur to bring the troops home.

The wild and woolly experience in the war with California was only one episode in the colorful life of Nellie Bush. She'd been a pilot on the Colorado since 1915 and was the only woman to have a license to operate a riverboat. She also was one of Arizona's first licensed airplane pilots. In 1920, she was elected to the Arizona legislature and served there for sixteen years.

A year after entering the legislature, she decided to enroll in law school at the University of Arizona. Early on, she demonstrated a genius for persuasion. Once she was banned from attending a class where the subject of rape was being discussed. She went to the dean and wanted to know if he'd ever heard of a case of rape where a woman wasn't involved. He hadn't, and Nellie returned triumphantly to class.

CHAPTER 42

An Inch'll Do

Old Arizona was an ideal place for a woman to find equality among the sexes. Women mavericks and adventurers straddled horses, prospected, ranched, filed on homesteads, and worked at jobs just like men. Eastern women oftentimes saw their Western sisters toiling in jobs normally held by men and mistakenly believed they needed emancipating.

A young ranch woman in Cochise County during the 1920s named Mary Kidder Rak, and her husband Charlie, discovered that she got along better with the cattle and he was a better cook. So they reversed roles.

Soon after, an Eastern lady visiting the ranch came upon Charlie working in the kitchen and, and seeing Mary outside feeding the calves, took exception to the arrangement. But Charlie explained matter-of-factly, "Mary would rather work with the cattle."

The Eastern visitor was determined to emancipate Mary from the chains or reatas that bound her to the corral and get her back in the kitchen where she belonged. Her solution was to point out the amenities one enjoyed in the East, including such contraptions as electric stoves, refrigerators, and washing machines— doodads that were guaranteed to make a woman want to spend her life in domesticity. But Mary stubbornly refused give up her life in the outdoors. She loved saddling up some cowpony and riding from sunup to sundown. So, she dismissed her friend's enticements by saying, "It wouldn't do any good to have all those appliances since there isn't any electricity at the ranch anyway."

"Why Mary!" her friend exclaimed. "I should think that more than anything else in the world you would want electricity."

Mary took off her wide-brimmed hat, wiped her brow, and replied, "More than anything else in the world—I want an inch of rain."

'Twas Once in the Saddle

CHAPTER 43

Those Old Irish Cowboy Songs

How many cowboys does it take to screw in a lightbulb? Two! One to screw in the bulb and another to write a song about how much they miss the old one!

Folks who gained all their knowledge about real cowboys from watching the Saturday afternoon matinees naturally figured the breed had been miraculously endowed with wonderful, mellifluous singing voices. The storyline was pure formula Western and there was always a clear distinction between the forces of good and evil. The good guys wore white hats and colorfully embroidered shirts; the bad guys wore dark hats and sneered a lot through bushy mustaches.

In the evening, after a hard day of chasing stampeding cows, deadly shootouts with desperados, enduring countless flesh wounds, and saving some helpless, shrinking violet in distress, the good guys could be found around the campfire, romanticizing the Old West in song. Roy, Gene, Tex, or Rex would strap on the ole guitar and the Sons of the Pioneers would suddenly materialize in the background to provide harmony. Even John Wayne tried his hand at being a singing cowboy, warbling tunes in his early oaters under the pseudonym of "Singin' Sandy."

As we grew older and cynicism set in, we learned not to always trust the guy in the white hat. So, we naturally assumed that real cowboys probably didn't sing either.

Fact is, many old-time cowboys did sing around the campfire. They didn't sound too pretty. Real cowpunchers never had time for singing lessons. Their untrained vocalizing sounded more like a burro with a bad cold than one of the crooning cowboys of Hollywood fame. But that didn't really matter. Singing was thought to soothe the restless cattle and there is no historical data to indicate that cows ever complained about the cacophonous noise. Besides, it was lonely work and the singing helped fight off the loneliness.

Real cowboys usually didn't accompany themselves on the guitar, preferring instead to sing *a capella*. "Besides," as one said, "the guitar is always off-key from my singing." Also, the life of a guitar on the range was brief. The elements made short work of such delicate instruments.

The songs they sang were usually old hymns or poems set to the popular tunes of the day. For example, the old 1890s classic that is often credited as being the first real cowboy song, "When the Work's All Done this Fall," was originally sung to the music of the popular tune, "After the Ball is Over." Most, however, were of other origins and the cowboys changed the words to fit their own surroundings.

American cowboys were a mulligan stew of ethnic groups. Cowboy singer-writer Katie Lee, in her authoritative book on cowboy music, *Ten Thousand Goddam Cattle*, tells of a cowboy friend, Shorty Mac, who describes cow country as having "so many different lingos floatin' on the breeze them pore cows prob'ly wondered what country they was in."

The Irish were well-represented in the Old West and they contributed richly to American cowboy music. Originally, many came to America to help build the Western railroads and when that work was done, drifted out into the cattle country looking for work. Their gregarious nature allowed them to fit comfortably into the boisterous, devil-may-care cowboy culture of the Old West. And they brought their songs with them.

Perhaps the best known was "Green Grow the Rushes Oh!" The American version was the old Texas favorite, "Green Grow the Lilacs." It's been claimed, erroneously, that the word *gringo* is derived from the song. It was said the Mexicans heard the Texans singing the song so frequently they began to refer to them as "Green Grows," later corrupted into *gringo*.

The roots to the classic cowboy song, "Whoopee Ti Yi Yo (Get Along Little Dogies)" have been traced back to the 1600s in Ireland. It began as the "Old Man's Lament" and told the story of a sailor who went off to sea for seven years, leaving behind a beautiful wife. He returned to find her with a young child that was "none of his own." In the song, he's trying to be philosophical as he rocks the cradle, saying that when a man goes off to sea and leaves a beautiful wife at home for seven years, she's bound to get into some mischief. Now there's an understanding fella.

The Irish cowboys changed the words to tell the story of driving dogies up the trail to Wyoming. A dogie, incidentally, is defined as a calf whose mother has died and whose father has run off with another cow. The song draws an interesting parallel between motherless calves and a fatherless child.

Another favorite old Irish ballad converted into a cowboy classic was the "Unfortunate Rake." It was first heard in the 1790s as an army song with lyrics that got more vulgar as the verses progressed. It tells the story of a young soldier dying from a well-known social disease acquired from one of the camp followers. The song spread to America about 1830 as the "Bad Girl's Lament."

It's been said that when the song arrived in cattle country, the words were considered too vulgar for cowboys to sing (??) so the soldiers, sailors, and bawdy women were replaced with more puritanical whiskey-drinkin', poker-playin' cowboys. The song became "The Cowboy's Lament" or perhaps better known as the "Streets of Laredo."

Another old tune is the "Educated Fellar or Zebra Dun." This one tells the story of a smooth-talking, well-mannered gentleman walking into a cow camp at suppertime, regaling the punchers with fancy, "jawbreakin' words," then asking to borrow a "nice, fat saddle hoss." Nobody loved a practical joke more than cowboys, especially when it was on somebody they perceived as being a greenhorn. So they saddled up an outlaw horse called the Zebra Dun. A Zebra Dun is a buckskin with dark, zebra-like stripes on his forelegs above his fetlocks. They were described by one old cowhand as being the "toughest, wickedest, most devilish-tempered brute that ever felt a cinch on his belly or crippled up a poor cow person."

The joke backfired as this educated cowboy commenced to ride the outlaw bronc easily. Just to show his disdain, he even rolled himself a cigarette and smoked it while sitting atop that bucking bronc. In the end, he showed the punchers that sometimes an "educated fellar ain't some plumb greenhorn."

The song is sung to the tune of the old Irish air, "The Son of a Gambolier." During the 1960s, the late legend of country western music, Marty Robbins, recorded a modern-day rendition of the song called, "The Cowboy in a Continental Suit."

Cowboy songs have their own particular charm. Many are sad songs, reflecting the loneliness of the life. They tell of lost friends, families, and sweethearts. Sometimes the wry humor of the cowboy sneaks into the words. Jim Bob Tinsley, cowboy raconteur, describes one such classic old tune, "Red River Valley," where the syntax resulted in a subtle double meaning. Methinks there is also a touch of good old Irish humor in these lyrics:

> *From this valley they say you are going;*
> *When you go, may your darlin' go too?*
> *Would you leave her behind unprotected,*
> *When she loves no other but you?*

CHAPTER 44

The Devil Made 'Em Do It!

Prescott's notorious "Whiskey Row" is one of Arizona's best-known bibulous Babylons. Even Prescottonians have a hard time remembering that its real name is Montezuma Street. The nickname comes from the early days when forty saloons flanked the west side of the street.

The row began at the Kentucky Bar, on corner of Goodwin and Montezuma and ran north all the way to the Depot House Saloon down near the Santa Fe Depot. With so many places to choose from, social imbibing was the favorite pastime of revelers.

It was customary each payday for thirsty cowboys to come to Prescott and head for the nearest saloon. As they used to say, "a cowboy and his money are soon partying." They began at the Kentucky Bar, "at the head of Whiskey Row," and ended up at the Depot House Saloon, "about forty drinks below."

Then, if they were really feeling macho, they would "set up, turn around" and try to drink their way back up to the other end. Thus was provided the inspiration for one of Arizona's most enduring legends and celebrated cowboy poems.

The late Yavapai County cowboy "Poet Lariat," Gail Gardner, penned the classic tale of two drunken cowboys named Sandy Bob and Buster Jig, who had a celebrated encounter with the Devil in the mountains outside of Prescott. The two had been on a wild spree on Whiskey Row and were riding back out to their ranch in the Sierra Prieta mountains, known locally as the "Sierry Petes," when the Devil jumped out of a hole and prepared to gather in their sinful souls.

In the Hollywood movies, cowboys would have gone for their six-shooters and filled the *Foul Fiend* full of lead. But this was the real West. So, instead, the irrepressible pair went for their lariats. Sandy Bob's rope caught ol' Lucifer by the horns and Buster Jig shook out his rawhide reata and tossed a loop around his hind legs. They stretched out the Devil on the ground, branded, ear-marked and pruned his horns. Then, for good measure, the two punchers necked him up to a blackjack oak tree and gave him the ultimate in humiliation—they tied knots in his forked tail.

Cowpunchers up in Yavapai County swear that if you ride those "Sierry Petes" at night and listen closely you can still hear that ol' Devil bellowin' and wailin' about the awful indignities he suffered at the hands of those two sinful cowboys.

The Sierry Petes
or, Tyin' Knots in the Devil's Tail

Away up high in the Sierry Petes
 Where the yeller pines grows tall
Ol' Sandy Bob and Buster Jig,
 Had a rodeer camp last fall.

Oh, they taken their hosses and runnin' irons
 And mabbe a dawg or two,
An' they 'lowed they'd brand all the long-yered calves,
 That come within their view.

And any old dogie that flapped long yeres,
 And didn't bush up by day,
Got his long yeres whittled an' his old scortched,
 In a most artistic way.

Now one fine day ol' Sandy Bob
 He throwed his seago down,
"I'm sick of the smell of burnin' hair,
 And I 'lows I'm a-goin' to town."

So they saddles up an' hits 'em a lope,
 Fer it warnt no sight of a ride,
And them was the days when a buckaroo
 Could ile up his inside.

Oh, they starts her in at the Kentucky Bar,
 At the head of Whiskey Row,
And they winds up down by the Depot House,
 Some forty drinks below.

They then sets up and turns around,
 And goes her the other way,
An' to tell you the gawd-forsaken truth,
 Them boys got stewed that day.

235

As they was a-ridin' back to camp
  A-packin' a pretty good load,
Who should they meet but the Devil himself,
  A-prancin down the road.

Sez he, "you ornery cowboy skunks,
  You'd better hunt yer holes,
Fer I've come up from Hell's rimrock
  To gather in yer souls."

Sez Sandy Bob, ol' Devil be damned,
  We boys is kinda tight,
But you ain't a-goin' to gather no cowboy souls,
  'Thout you has some kind of a fight.

So Sandy Bob punched a hole in his rope,
  And he swang her straight and true,
He lapped it on to the Devil's horns,
  An' he taken his dallies, too.

Now Buster Jig was a riata man,
  With his gut-line coiled up neat,
So he shaken her out an' he built him a loop,
  An' he lassed the Devil's hind feet.

Oh, they stretched him out an' they tailed him down,
  While the irons was a-gettin' hot,
They cropped and swaller-forked his yeres,
  Then they branded him up a lot.

They pruned him up with a de-hornin' saw,
  An' they knotted his tail fer a joke,
They then rid off and left him there,
  Necked to a black-jack oak.

If you're ever up high in the Sierry Petes,
  And you hear one hell of a wail
You'll know it's that Devil a-bellerin' around
  About them knots in his tail.

— by Gail I. Gardner, aka "Buster Jig"

CHAPTER 45

Cowboy Poetry Has a Message

Cowboy poetry has been recently discovered by the masses. Cowboy poets with wide-brimmed hats, high-heeled boots, and drooping mustaches appear regularly on national television regaling audiences with home-spun stories put to rhyme. Actually, cowboy poets have been around longer than cowboy singers. Admittedly, a few cowboys did attempt to sing *a capella* around the campfire but, since nobody knew the words to that, they settled for reciting poetry instead.

The only cowboys who enjoyed the luxury of having a guitar around the campfire were such stalwarts as Roy, Gene, Tex, and Rex. The rest had to settle for singing without an instrument. Most claimed it didn't really matter since the musical instrument was always off-key from their singing anyway.

Most of the stories set to rhyme tell about the life of the cowboy, something about ranch work, or about the land where cowboys work. One of the oldest cowboy poems, according to Slim Chance, came from a cowhand and his wife over in Apache County. It all started when she decided to enter a slogan contest the Carnation Milk Company was holding. She penned the following lines:

Carnation's the best milk in the land
Comes ready to use in a little red can.

Her husband was going into town for supplies, so she gave it to him to mail. Several weeks passed by and she'd gotten no response from her entry, so she asked him one day if he'd remembered to mail it.

"I shore did," he replied! "I thought it was real good, but needed a kicker so I wrote in a couple of lines."

"What did you add?" she asked apprehensively.

He smiled proudly and replied:

No tits to pull, no hay to pitch
Just punch two holes in the son of a bitch.

And that's how, according to Slim Chance, cowboy poetry got started.

CHAPTER 46

The Misunderstood Cowboy

The working cowboy was the ancestral figure that produced the grand image created by pulp writers and movie makers of the two-fisted, rowdy, hell-raisin' knight in dusty leather, the singing cowboy, John Wayne, and the Marlboro Man. Easterners were fascinated with the wild and woolly West, especially the free-spirited cowboys, but most of their knowledge came from shoot-em-up dime novels.

In the early days, they usually got their first glimpse of the Old West through the window of a passenger train. They would seldom leave the safety of the rail car, preferring instead to observe cowboys from behind a glass window. After all, according to the pulp Westerns, cowboys were only part-human. And, cowboys were aware of this public perception, too. They certainly didn't want to disappoint their visitors and were always happy to oblige.

Innocent, god-fearing cowpunchers like Shorty and Slim would ride into towns like Two Gun, Arizona, on payday and the first thing they'd do is stop by the church and visit the parson. Then they'd go over to the ice cream parlor for a glass of cold lemonade before heading for the library to check out some books or study their Boy Scout manuals, or maybe even play a little Monopoly. When the westbound train would pull into Two Gun at high noon, Slim would say,

"Shorty, I see the train is a-comin'. I guess we'd better have 'nother gunfight so them Easterners won't be disappointed and can have somethin' to talk about when they get home."

"Say, Slim," Shorty would reply, "this time I'll give you a flesh wound in the left shoulder and you put a crease my arm with yore old six-shooter."

"Jest go a little easy on that shoulder, Shorty, you've already put seventeen holes in there since them Easterners started comin'."

Sure enough, the train would halt in a cloud of steam, and the passengers would peer out the window just in time to see those two galoots square off in the dusty street. Little did Shorty and Slim know at the time, but many years later, in movie-set towns like Old Tucson and Rawhide, cowboy actors would recreate those legendary shootouts for tourists. Fortunately for today's gunfighters, blank ammunition is used.

Poor Shorty and Slim didn't have such amenities for their gun brawls. They just wanted to maintain the rootin'-tootin' image of the cowboy and shot the hell out of each other time after time. Soon as the train would pull out, the boys would resume their monopoly game or maybe go to a prayer meeting or something like that.

Despite those occasional sorties into town to entertain the tourists and maintain their image, cowboys were range. Badger Clark, Poet Lariat from South Dakota, captured this feeling in his classic poem, "From Town."

From Town

We are the children of the open and we hate
    the haunts o' men,
But we had to come to town to get the mail.
We was ridin' home at daybreak —'cause
    the air is cooler then,
All 'cept one of us that stopped behind in jail.

Shorty's nose won't bear paradin',
    Bill's off eye is darkly fadin',
All our toilets show a touch of disarray,
For we have found that city life
    is a constant round of strife
And we ain't the breed for shyin' from a fray.

Chant your warwhoop, pardners dear,
    while the east turns pale with fear
And the chaparral is tremblin' all aroun'.
For we're wicked to the marrer,
    we're a midnight dream of terror
When we're ridin' up the rocky trail from town!

We acquired our hasty temper from our friend,
    the centipede.
From the rattlesnake we learnt to guard our rights.
We have gathered fightin' pointers from the famous
    bronco steed
And the bobcat teached us reppertee that bites.

So when some high-collared herrin'
    jeered the garb that I was wearin',
Twasn't long till we had got where talkin' ends.
And he et his illbred chat,
    with a sauce of derby hat,
While my merry pardners entertained his friends.

Sing 'er out, my buckaroos!
        Let the desert hear the news.
Tell the stars the way we rubbed the haughty down.
We're the fiercest wolves a-prowlin'
        and it's just our night for howlin'
When we're ridin' up the rocky trail from town.

Since the days that Lot and Abram
        split the Jordan range in halves,
Just to fix it so their punchers wouldn't fight.
Since old Jacob skinned his dad-in-law
        for six year's crop of calves,
And then hit the trail for Canaan in the night,
There has been a taste for battle
        'mong the men that follow cattle
And a love for doin' things that's wild and strange.
And the warmth of Laban's words
        when he missed his speckled herds
Still is useful in the language of the range.

Sing 'er out, my bold coyotes!
        leather fists and leather throats,
For we wear the brand of Ishm'el like a crown.
We're the sons o' desolation,
        we're the outlaws of creation—
Ee-yow! a ridin' up the rocky trail from town!

242

CHAPTER 47

Cowboy Rap

Recently I decided to write a cowboy poem that dealt with the latest fad to hit the music world—rap. After listening to a couple of rappers, I figured rap was nothing but cowboy poetry speeded up with lots of dirty words added. My twelve-year-old son, Roger, gave me a few tips on body motion (somehow or other I missed the Hula-Hoop craze) and I was on my way to becoming a cowboy rapper.

Cowboy Rap

If you wanta be a cowboy
Let me tell ya what to do.
Gotta get yourself an outfit
And you'll be a buckaroo.

Ya gotta have boots
And a fancy cowboy hat.
And a belt with yer name
Stamped on the back.

A bright-colored shirt
Is just what ya need
To become a part
Of the cowboy breed.

Them tight-fittin' jeans
Might feel kinda funny
But they'll always attract
Some long-legged bunny.

Ya need a silver buckle
To be real dap
But if ya can't afford one
Then wear a hub cap.

Ya gotta have a pickup
Bumper stickers on the back
And in the rear window
Ya hang a gun rack.

Ya don't need a horse
And ya don't need a saddle.
Ya don't need to know
A single thing about cattle.

Ya learn to rap real slow
And before ya even know it
They might start to call you
A cowboy poet.

CHAPTER 48

When in Doubt . . .
Go Ahead

Expanding the truth is a cherished tradition among cowboy raconteurs. It's also considered coarse manners to correct a liar. With that disclaimer, I'll admit to writing this poem shortly after the temperature hit 122 degrees in the shade on June 26, 1990.

I'd been in Flagstaff that morning and knew that when the snow started melting, it was going to be a hot one up there, too. By the time I got to Phoenix, the temperature was approaching 122 degrees. My air conditioner had quit and the swimming pool had turned to Gatorade. There was nothing left to do but sit down and write a cowboy poem.

I thought about all those newcomers who memorize the day and the hour they arrived in Arizona to stay so they can lord it over their less fortunate neighbors who moved here later. I worked out a formula to determine seniority status.

Another group was the long time residents who suffer from the "I coulda' bought it for" syndrome. I especially wanted to chastise the chamber of commerce for imposing the slogan, "Summer Heat is No Sweat" on our parched throats. Especially since some chamber members spend summers in San Diego. Before this introduction gets longer than the poem, let's remember our motto: "When in Doubt . . . Go Ahead."

Bragging is a Cherished Right

Bragging is a cherished right
  And correcting liars is a sin.
If something didn't happen exactly this way,
  That's how it could, or should have been.

Arizonans love to exaggerate,
  The facts they do enhance.
And when they start palaverin,'
  First liar never has a chance.

This place is so great one can't help but exaggerate
  The wondrous wonders a bit.
I caught myself tellin' the truth yesterday
  But, thank god, I was able to lie my way out of it.

Natives are known to bemoan and lament
  Recalling days of yore
Of hot real estate deals that came and went
  Crying "way back then, when I coulda bought it for . . ."

Seniority status comes highest to those
  Who were the earliest to come hither.
Twenty years beats ten and ten beats five,
  But one summer beats a pair of winters.

Promoters boast with civic pride
    That summer heat's "no sweat."
It's 110 in the shade but we've got it made
    Because it's a dry heat instead of a wet.

Critics claim summers are too derned hot,
    But they got the whole thing wrong.
Summers ain't so sizzling hot,
    They just last too doggoned long.

Over in Mesa it once got so hot
    That a farmer's cornfield started to pop.
A herd of cattle in a pasture nearby
    Thought it was snow so they froze up and died.

But the blistering heat didn't spoil the meat.
    At least, so the story's been told.
They packed 'em in popcorn and shipped 'em to market
    Claiming that's how they kept the meat cold.

Old-timers out in Gila Bend
    Like to tell a tale
About a sinful prospector
    Who died and went straight down to hell.

But he got a chill and became quite ill
    And feared he'd never get well.
So he walked right up to the devil bold
    Sayin', "this place for me is too dern cold."

So the devil asked, "what can I do
    To make this place more agreeable for you?"
"Turn up the heat," the sourdough replied.
    "It was hotter 'en this up there where I died."

Six inches of rain in this desert terrain
    Is no reason to take heart.
A six-inch rain is still cause to complain
    Because the drops measured six inches apart.

There once was a time, the old-timers tell
    When, for seven long years, no moisture fell.
But they didn't despair for they knew all too well
    That it always rains after a dry spell.

Our mountains are higher, our rivers are drier,
    Our fish never learned how to swim.
Our sunsets are redder and our duststorms are better.
    They'll bury you right up to your chin.

A cowboy named Smiley was out ridin one day
    When a great big duststorm came a-blowin his way.
His partner named Lefty, who was a very good hand
    Found him at sunrise, buried nose-deep in sand.

He spat out a mouthful
    Still a-smilin of course,
Sayin, "Go get a shovel Lefty,
    Cause I'm still sittin atop my ole horse."

When the temperature hits 122
    Breaking records that couldn't be beat,
We can always take great comfort in knowing
    That it is, after all, a very dry heat.

CHAPTER 49

And If It Wasn't, It Should'a Been

Out in cattle country, cows were considered "hairy banknotes" and stealing them was the same as taking money. This was especially true if the culprit was a stranger in those parts, or a hated "nester." He might get a suspended sentence from the limb of the nearest cottonwood tree if he got caught putting his brand on some rancher's cows.

Still, contrary to popular myth, cattlemen didn't always hang rustlers in the Old West. Neighbors were particularly reluctant to press charges as long as the pilfering wasn't flagrant. The following poem is based on a true event. And if it wasn't, it should have been.

Eatin' Your Own Beef

Thou Shalt Not Covet Thy Neighbors Cows
Was the Eleventh Commandment on the range.
But petty pilfering among close neighbors
Wasn't so unusual or all that strange.

These two old cowmen named Shorty and Slim
  Had been neighbors for many a year
But they hadn't much time for socializing
  Except for an occasional beer.

Then Shorty rode out to his neighbor's one day
  Saying "Slim, let's celebrate.
We've been friends for thirty-five years.
  Let's commemorate the historic date."

"I'll host the fiesta at my ole ranch
  And I'll cook up the beef.
It'll be the biggest bash you ever saw,
  More grub than you could eat in a week."

So Shorty threw a big barbecue,
  Folks came from miles to celebrate.
'Twas the biggest shindig in them parts,
  He must have fed nearly half of the state.

It was getting purty late in the evening,
  And they'd all had plenty to drink
When Slim laughed and slapped his host on the back
  Saying "Shorty, I've got a confession to make."

"Now we've been neighbors
  For thirty-five years and I'm confessing now
That I've never yet in all that time
  Eaten one of my own cows."

Shorty smiled and gazed upon
  Those heaps of bar-be-que.
He turned to his friend and said with a grin,
  "Well now Slim, I've got a confession, too.

"You say you've never once, in thirty-five years,
  Ever eaten one of your own cows.
I reckon tonite makes up fer lost time
  'Cause Slim you sure are eatin' 'em now."

One of my favorite Arizona cowboy poets is Rolf Flake of Gilbert. His historic roots grow deep in the state and he savvies this land and its people. Rolf's family settled on the Colorado Plateau in the 1870s and is credited with providing half the name to the town of Snowflake. His poem, "A Frog Strangler and a Gully Washer," gives a fitting description of rainfall in this dry land.

A Frog Strangler and a Gully Washer

An Arizona cowboy chanced to visit
  Once "back East."
And while there it happened that
  He was invited to a "feast."

While visitin' with the "natives"
  As he waited for things to begin,
He was the "center of attention"
  And they wanted to question him.

'Cause they knew he was different,
  To them he seemed quite strange.
I guess they'd never seen a cowboy
  Who'd just come in off the range.

They asked him about the rainfall
  And if it wasn't awful dry
Back there in Arizona.
  He said yes—at times it did get dry.

But they got quite specific
  And asked if he could tell
Just how many "inches" of moisture
  Through the whole year might have "fell."

He allowed that six or seven inches
    Throughout the whole year would do it.
They said that sure wasn't very much,
    It was terribly dry—they knew it.

"Well," he drawled, "I'll have to admit,
    That fer a year it isn't much at all.
But I'm here to tell you somethin'—
    You oughta be there on the day it falls."

— Reprinted from *Western Verse or Worse*,
by Rolf Flake. Copyright © 1989

Rolf Flake has been around ranching all his life and claims there's only three things that put fear into ranch people—bad weather, bad markets, and having to pay a visit to the banker.

The "Eyes" Have It

Well, I went to see the Banker
* To borrow me some "dough."*
I went with fear and trembling—
* Afraid he'd tell me "No."*

But that Banker, he surprised me—
* Said, "I'll tell you what I'll do.*
I have one glass eye, if you can guess which
* I'll just make that loan to you."*

I'm sure that he had done this before
* With many an unsuspecting "catch."*
And I'm sure he'd won more times than lost
* 'Cause his eyes were so well matched.*

Which eye was glass? How could I tell?
* But then I saw the light!*
"It's that one sir, I'm sure it is.
* The one that's on your right."*

Well that Banker he was startled
* That I could tell so fast.*
Said, "I'll keep my word—you got the loan—
* But tell me, how did you guess?"*

"Well, sir," I said, " 'twas easy—
* I figured it in this fashion—*
The one on the right—the glass one—
* Has just a glimmer of 'compassion.' "*

— Reprinted from *Western Verse or Worse,*
by Rolf Flake. Copyright © 1989

Cowboy poetry is to "real" poetry what Louis L'Amour is to Western literature. It just don't get no respect. A notable exception is Baxter Black of Brighton, Colorado. Bax has managed to achieve considerable respect outside the genre.

Baxter Black is also the only cowboy poet who can honestly claim to make a living at it. He was raised in New Mexico and has been around cowboys all his life. His humor accurately mirrors the life and times of people who make their living off the land. Most of his material is written *for* cowboys instead of *about* them. Still, folks who don't know which end of a cow gets up first, enjoy his unique brand of poetry. Bax has appeared several times with Johnny Carson on the "Tonight Show." How many "real" poets can make that claim?

Baxter has also done a great service to Western historiana by paying homage to one of the most maligned of critters—the chicken. We've honored the great men and women of the Old West. We've recognized a few great horses; even heaped praise on a couple of steers like Old Blue and Sancho. But in our haste, we've overlooked the lowly chicken.

Why honor the chicken, you ask? Because every little boy or girl who wants to grow up and punch cows has to learn to rope first. The true mark of a cowboy isn't the boots, hat, horse, or pickup—it's the ability to handle a lariat. You have to start when you're young and, when you're a little tyke, it's hard to outsmart the dogs and cats. And the calves are too big. The only thing in the barnyard dumb enough to let you practice is a chicken. The point is, every good roper probably owes their skill to some mangy chicken and it's about time they get the recognition they deserve.

In Defense of the Chicken

Everyone says they love chicken,
    Ambrosia sent from above.
But nobody loves a chicken,
    A chicken ain't easy to love.

It's hard to housebreak a chicken.
    They just don't make very good pets.
You might teach one bird imitations
    But that's 'bout good as it gets.

Mentally, they're plumb light-headed
    And never confused by the facts.
That's why there's no seeing-eye chickens,
    Guard chickens or trained chicken acts.

And everything tastes like chicken
    From rattlesnake meat to fried bats.
It's got this anonymous flavor;
    I figger they're all Democrats.

They say this ignoble creature
    With his intellect unrefined
And lack of civilized manners
    Has little to offer mankind.

But let me suggest, the chicken
    Had two contributions to make;
The first one is the pecking order,
    The second is the chicken fried steak!

— Reprinted from *Fractured Cowboy Poetry*
by Baxter Black. Copyright © 1992

When the brandin', doctorin', and castratin' was all done, it was custom in cow country to have a feast and the main item on the menu was rocky mountain oysters. Any greenhorn who happened by for dinner was sure to be offered a plateful. Most swore they were delicious, until someone told them what it was they were eatin'.

Baxter Black's poem, "The Oyster, " reflects on those occasions when two people of diverse backgrounds are conversing and one is talking about one thing and the other is hearing something altogether different.

Picture, if you will, a scene inside a cafe in Springerville, Arizona. A local cowboy is taking his lady friend from Chesapeake Bay, Maryland to lunch.

The Oyster

The sign upon the cafe wall said
    OYSTERS: fifty cents.
"How quaint," the blue-eyed sweetheart said,
    with some bewildermence.
"I didn't know they served such fare
    up here upon the Plain?"
"Oh, sure," her cowboy date replied,
    "we're really quite urbane."

"I would guess they're Chesapeake or Blue Point,
    don't you think?"
"No ma'am, they're mostly hereford cross . . .
    and usually they're pink."
But I've been cold, so cold myself,
    what you say could be true.
And if a man looked close enough,
    their points could sure be blue!

She said, "I gather them myself,
    out on the bay alone.
I pluck them from the murky depths
    and smash them with a stone!"
The cowboy winced
    imagining a calf with her beneath.
"Me, I use a pocketknife
    and yank 'em with my teeth."

"Oh, my," she said, "you animal!
    How crude and unrefined!
Your masculine assertiveness
    sends shivers up my spine!
But I prefer a butcher knife
    too dull to really cut.
I wedge it in on either side
    and crack it like a nut!"

"I pry them out. If they resist,
    sometimes I use the pliers
Or even grandpa's pruning shears
    if that's what it requires!"
The hair stood out on the cowboy's neck,
    His stomach gave a whirl.
He'd never heard such grisly talk,
    especially from a girl!

"I like them fresh," the sweetheart said,
    and laid her menu down.
Then ordered oysters for them both
    when the waiter came around.
The cowboy smiled gamely,
    though her words stuck in his craw.
But he finally fainted dead away when she said,
    "I'll have mine raw!"

— Reprinted from *Fractured Cowboy Poetry*
by Baxter Black. Copyright © 1992

CHAPTER 50

Legends in Levis

Legends in Levis is a poem set to music I wrote several years ago as a tribute to the men and women who have given America its grandest image:

Legends in Levis

Call 'em Legends in Levis
    The last paladins,
The idols of an age
    Turned to legends, my friends.

'Though the trail dust has settled
    And the cowtowns are gone,
Their ghosts ride the range
    And the legend lives on.

It was down in South Texas
    Where the legend began,
Gatherin' wild cattle
    On the old Rio Grande.

They drove 'em to Kansas
*   On the old Chisholm Trail*
To Abilene town
*   And the K and P Rail.*

The legends grew tall
*   As they spread o'er the West,*
Knight errants on horseback
*   On a romantic quest.*

They could ride tornados,
*   Rope anything that wore hair,*
Fight grizzlies bare-knuckled
*   And plum devil-may-care.*

But the real life of the cowboy
*   Apart from the myth,*
Was toilin' in the hot sun
*   Or a blue norther' wind.*

Ridin' and ropin' was
*   Their main stock in trade,*
No prouder profession
*   The legend was made.*

The wide open spaces
*   They claimed as their own,*
The freest hired hand
*   This world's ever known.*

Homeless as a poker chip
*   And restless as the wind,*
His workbench was a saddle
*   A good horse, his best friend.*

They rode hell-for-leather
Across this great land,
The trails they left
Are cut deep in the sand.

They'll never plow under
What the cowhand stood for,
Those hard-ridin' heros
Of legend and lore.

Call 'em Legends in Levis
The last paladins,
The idols of an age
Turned to legends, my friends.

'Though the trail dust has settled
And the cowtowns are gone,
Their ghosts ride the range
And the legend lives on.

CHAPTER 51

Country Music has a Message, Too!

I think it's important to point out that Western music and cowboy poetry are unique and shouldn't be confused with country music. In recent years, country music has abandoned its roots and crossed over into other fields. It's pretty hard to define country music, but still the lyrics remain deeply concerned with traditional values.

Country songs reach across the wide spectrum of society. A few years ago, David Allen Coe and Steve Goodman pointed out that for a country song to be perfect it must include something about dogs, like old Shep, mamas, farms, trucks, trains, prison, and getting drunk. They managed to cram all that into one verse.

Country songs also play heavily on the emotions of the downtrodden. For example: What do you get when you play a country song backwards?

1. You sober up; 2. You get out of jail; 3. Your wife comes back home; and 4. You get your truck back! No hidden satanic messages there!

Country music songs are usually characterized by rural corn and catchy titles with convoluted puns. Double meanings are a staple and they usually tend towards the sordid side of life.

Some examples of these inspiring titles include: "Now I Lay Me Down to Cheat," "I'm Seein' Double and Feelin' Single," "She Sang with Me but Played with the Band," and "It Got Around to Me that You Been Gettin' Around with Him."

A dose of religion is always good for a country song, as demonstrated by "Drop Kick Me Jesus through the Goal Post of Life." The subject of two-timin' your partner is dealt with in the songs "You Can't Have Your Kate and Edith Too," and "You're Out Doing What I'm Here Doing Without." Blaming each other is a common theme, as evidenced by "It's Your Fault the Kids are Ugly."

Sociological family issues are discussed in the country classic "You Don't Have to Be a Weightlifter to Have Dumbbells for Kids." Macho country double-entendre is highlighted in the tune "If I Said You had a Beautiful Body Would You Hold It Against Me." The Pshaw Award for Bad Taste goes to "I Used to Kiss Your Lips but Now It's All Over."

By now, I'm sure you get the idea. For those who might want to try their hand at writing a country song, I'll suggest a few catchy titles (that's really the hardest part). The operative word here is hook! All you need to do is add a few lines.

Using daddy and mama in the title is a surefire guarantee hit. How about "When They Operated on Daddy, They Opened Up Mama's Male." Or, you might prefer something more earthy like "The Man from the Gas Company Turned My Woman On." This title begs to ask the question "Can a Boy Who Comes from Buffalo Ever Find Happiness with a Girl Who Comes from Normal Parents?"

Cowboy bars are the most democratic places on earth. Everyone is welcome except pacifists, thus inspiring this title: "You Caught My Eye Last Night—Right After Your Boyfriend Knocked It Out." And, last but not least, country yuppies are dealt with in the classic title without words, "You Said You were Out Joggin' but You were Runnin' Around on Me!"

Tha-tha-that's all folks!

Marshall Trimble's *Special Warranty*

If you're not completely satisfied with this book, return it to me, along with a check for the exact amount you paid for it. Within five days, I will cheerfully return your check.